Run From A Scarecrow

Irene Bennett Brown

WISE WOLF
BOOKS

WISE WOLF BOOKS
An Imprint of Wolfpack Publishing
wisewolfbooks.com
9850 S. Maryland Parkway, Suite A-5 #323, Las Vegas, Nevada 89183

Cover design by Wise Wolf Books

Paperback ISBN 978-1-957548-77-7
eBook ISBN 978-1-957548-73-9

With much affection, this book is dedicated to my Kansas and Missouri kin.

Run From A Scarecrow

Chapter One

It's over, Hank Hedin thought. He lay stiff and sweating on his corn shuck mattress, as though he had taken part in the birthing in the room below.

The infant bawled lustily. Hank swung his sturdy shoulders off the cot, close to the plank floor, to listen. Hearing Pa's bleak, "Ye got 'nother girl, Ninette," Hank groaned and furrowed tan fingers through his sandy-red hair.

Five, now! He sat up in bed and glared through the dawn gloom at his sisters, four abed, on the other side of the loft. I ought to light out, he thought. I ought to catch one of them freight trains heading west, to somewhere where there's other *boys.* There'd be good huntin' and fishin' out West, too, he told himself yearningly, better than rabbits and coons and old yellow catfish.

Hank threw back his comforter and got up. He was sick of she-folk and she-doings!

"Chore time, Hank," August Hedin bellowed suddenly. "Got a newborn babe down here needs freshenin' up. We're outta water—git yonder to the well 'fore you see to the critters."

"Comin', Pa," Hank answered, shrugging a suspender onto his shoulder.

The sun had already spiked through the morning mist and a golden light lay over the hill farm. Hank set the oak bucket on the stone curb of the well, took a deep breath, and kept walking, his bare toes curling away from the cold ground. Johanna could get the water, he told himself.

A nudge of conscience reminded him that Johanna, the oldest, would more than have her hands full this morning. Book-learner Elsa could get it, then, he argued with himself. Or Clover and Dixie, the twins. They were big enough to hay the horses, Lucy and Sal, and see to the chickens, too.

He couldn't take any more. Somethin' musta blighted the boy-seed around here fourteen years ago, Hank decided. A deep, quivering sigh shook him. Fourteen years was too long to live without knowing a single other fellow his own age! Ever since he had started attending Baldy School around the hill when he was seven, all the other pupils had been girls. The school year just past, his last, the Kinlay twins had attended, but they were just babies.

Hank hastened through the garden patch, a dead place this time of year. He crossed the stubbled cornfield and dropped into a gully choked with naked walnut trees. "Ain't hardly seen much of Missoura, even," he grumbled to himself.

"Go on back, May," he ordered the brown hound trailing at his heels. "I'm thinking—I'm thinking to have myself a real journeyin' good time. You ain't fit enough for that."

For an instant, Hank almost wanted to follow May's heavy form back toward the house. Then he whipped about, stuck out his chin, and kept going.

As Hank's long legs took him farther and farther from home, anticipation grew inside him. Might be we have neighbors I didn't know about, he thought to himself. Movers, just come. It isn't likely. But chorin' and grubbin' out rocks, and fetching water and wood does keep me frightful busy, so how would I know? I would near give my soul for a friend!

To drown out the lonely quiet of his journey, Hank started to sing. It was a cowboy song Mamma had learned somewhere:

> *"Come, all you melancholy folks*
> *Wherever you may be,*
> *I'll sing you about the cowboy*
> *Whose life is light and free..."*

For a long time he had wanted to be a cowboy. That's what he would do out West.

After he had crossed Lightning Creek on the flatboat ferry, hours later, the country was new to Hank. His legs begged for rest. He dropped under a poplar tree. With care he carved his name and the date in the bark with his pearl-handled jackknife: "HANK HEDIN. MARCH 10, 1891." He started to add, "GONE WEST," thought better of it, and put the knife back in his pocket.

~

THE SUN RODE HIGH AS HE MOVED ON. HIS STOMACH ached from emptiness. A black bass would taste good, but he had no hook or string. He turned his pockets wrong side out: One match from the precious block Mamma kept in a tin box and his jackknife. His sigh was loud in the woods. Why didn't I bring vittles? he thought. I'm as bare of necessaries as the new baby girl at home— and I want to go West!

Climbing a hill thick with young hickory and elm trees, Hank thought of the family. They'd be sitting down to dinner about now, Pa and the girls. Mamma and the new baby would be sleeping. Thinking how good Johanna's hot cornbread always smelled made him feel dizzy. His steps slowed.

Right now he ought to go home and take his licking. Hank hesitated. He looked longingly toward the west. But he knew he couldn't do it. Hank turned sadly but resolutely toward home again.

He started to sing, with less heart now for the words:

> "Saddle up, saddle up, the boss'll
>   holler out,
> When we're camped by the Pecos strea—"

He broke off, seeing the cave. How close he had come to missing it. The mouth of the cave was barely visible through the tangle of brush. When he went by the first time, he hadn't seen it.

As though a net had been thrown over him, drawing him in, Hank moved toward the cave. He hesitated just outside, twisted a dead stub of a limb from a shrub by the cave opening, and in a moment was able to light the frayed end of it with his match.

Hank stooped to enter and an owl flew out of the entrance just inches above his head. His heart thudded in his ears. He was instantly aware of the gloom inside the cave. The torch in his hand began to glow. Hank waited, gathering courage, then crept forward with the stealth of a panther. The rock floor was slippery. All about him was silence except for the trickle of water over rock.

After a time, the limestone walls drew away and Hank found himself in a large underground room. "Ho!" he said, then jumped at the startling clearness of his voice. He halted beside a black pool in the middle of the cavern floor, and, kneeling, examined the skeleton of a small animal at the pool's edge.

Hank moved on, the mystery of the unknown tugging at him. Time stopped as he wandered from the main cave into another passageway leading off to his left, and then into another branching away from that. "If you had a lick o' sense, you'd go back this minute—" he cautioned himself in a whisper.

It wasn't easy to see, now, he noticed. Unable to heed his better judgment, Hank moved on through the inky interior of the cave. Suddenly his toe struck rock and pain shot through his foot. Teeth clenched, and the injured foot tight in his right hand, Hank hopped wildly. On the third turn, his good foot slipped, the torch sailed away, and he landed hard on his back. The torch flickered out, plunging him into darkness.

Hank sat up, biting his lip. Now, which way is which? he wondered. Had he come from over that way? Or from over there? If only it wasn't so dark!

Maybe if he just turned around—Hank eased himself onto his hands and knees and began to crawl. After a few feet his fingers found the sharp edge of a precipice. With a cry, he backed away. Not that way! Not that way! In a moment, he began to breathe more easily, and he crept slowly in the opposite direction. Suddenly, he was filled with panic! Except for the cliff side, he seemed to be surrounded by huge boulders. How could it be? He got here, there had to be a way out!

Hank found the sharp edge of the precipice again. Lying on his stomach, he swung his arm down over the edge—maybe it was just a short drop. His fingers clawed empty space. Resisting an urge to howl like May, Hank drew back from the cliff edge, panting. What could he do? Pa and Mamma wouldn't know where he'd gone off to. He could die in here, starve to death, if—

"Help!" Hank screamed. "Somebody, get me outta here! Please!"

Hugging his knees, Hank yelled until his throat felt raw. Nobody could hear me, he told himself. Probably I sound like a fool yelling from the bottom of a barrel. Might as well look it in the eye—a body laid out for a coffin isn't any more done for than I am. Hank swiped at his eyes and yelled louder.

Then he heard a rustling sound. He clamped his lips and waited, scarcely breathing. The sound came again, closer. In a voice so edged with fear it hardly sounded like his own, Hank cried, "Somebody there? Here I am, behind these boulders. Can't—can't get myself out—"

Maybe it was a panther. Peering wildly about, Hank saw a small moving light. He yelled again.

The wait seemed endless. Hank shivered uncontrollably, the thick feeling in his throat threatening to stifle him. Then the light was close and a hand, warm and real, found his and pulled.

A choking sound escaped Hank, half laughter, half

sob. "You didn't talk up so I was scared you was a panther," he said, getting to his feet, more than happy to follow the lead of the hand. "Hold on now, can't hardly see, your light's so poor. Let me keep up with you—I reckon we have to shinny between a couple boulders *somewhere*. There's an awful falling-off place—you know about it?"

There was still no comment from his rescuer. "How'd you come to hear me?" Hank asked. "Do you live close by?" Realizing that again he would not be answered, Hank's pulse raced. *Who* was on the body end of this hand he was hanging onto for dear life? Somebody strong, a man or boy. Somebody as surefooted in this cave as a billy goat on Bluestone Mountain. But if he had a tongue, why didn't he use it?

After a time, they came to the opening of the cave. Hank drew a sharp breath when he saw more clearly the tall boy he followed. He was bone-thin and as mangy-looking as a coyote. He wore a few tattered scraps of cloth, and on his feet small animal skins were laced. Hank pulled his arm free and stopped. "Who are you?" he asked in a thin voice.

The boy motioned with his hand. Hank hastened by him. "You sure enough ain't related to my waggle-tongue sisters," he mumbled. "Wait!" he cried, seeing the other turning back.

"I'm obliged," Hank told him. "Wish I knew who I owe my thanks to. Say!" he exclaimed as realization dawned on him, "you can't talk, can you? You'd talk to me if you could, wouldn't you?" In the gloom Hank saw a flash of teeth as the other boy smiled his answer.

"Leastways, you can hear and understand me," Hank said. He dug the jackknife out of his pocket and held it out to the other. "It ain't much. But it's all I got to give you for savin' my life." After a slight hesitation, the boy snatched the knife from his palm.

In the dim light, Hank could make out the working of the other's full lips as he tried to speak. It hurt to watch. Hank lowered his eyes. "Don't," he said. "Ain't no need to say nothin' to me." When he looked up, the other boy was gone. Gone without a sound.

"Come back, come—" Hank sighed. Better not try to follow, he told himself. Next time you might not get found. Hank hurried outside, wishing he was home already.

An early star sparkled just over the stone chimney when he got there. As he trudged up the hill, worry gnawed at him. Pa would be angry, and had a right to be. "May," Hank called softly, "Come here, girl." She came slowly. For a long time, Hank stood in the yard under the big pine tree rubbing the dog's long velvet ears. Then he went in.

PA SAT BY THE FIRE IN THE STRAIGHT-BACKED CHAIR he'd made for himself. He looked up as Hank entered, and his face above his red-gold beard made Hank think of a cyclone brewing. Johanna, a tiny bundle clutched in her arms, left her rocker swinging and quietly herded Elsa and the twins toward Mamma's room.

"Hank's in tolerable trouble, ain't he, Sister?" Clover asked, worrying a dark curl around her forefinger. Johanna quieted her and closed the door after them.

"Ye been gone," Pa accused, "all day. I sent you for water—"

"I'm sorry, Pa," Hank said quietly. "I shouldn't oughtta done it, but—" With his gaze fastened to the flinty blue under Pa's caterpillar-like eyebrows, Hank tried to explain where he had gone and why. He said nothing about the cave-boy; he would save that for a time when Pa was in a fitter mood. As he talked, Hank's circling toe caught a splinter, but, except for a slight intake of breath, he didn't show it. He was sickeningly aware that when Pa's anger passed, he would laugh heartily about a boy who'd had a strong notion to go out West but was home again by nightfall. He'd brought in on himself, though, Hank decided.

Pa got up when Hank was finished. "Yer mamma is feeling poorly. We'll go out to the barn." His voice was as gloomy as the cave.

Later, in bed, Hank remembered the cave-boy. His fingers unconsciously traced the stripes of pain left on his thigh by the whipping Pa had given him in the barn.

How come that boy didn't have a whit of trouble finding his way out of the cave? he wondered. Why does he wear such strange trappings? He looked like he might even live right there, but how could he, in that black old cave! And how come? I have to see him again. I have to. I'll go back and look for him, first chance I can get away without getting Pa het up again.

"Field is finished, Pa," Hank yelled one evening several days later. Dusk had settled in the hills, and there was just enough light left to see to unhitch.

"Poor girls," Hank crooned, leading the mud-colored horses away from the knotty log he had used to harrow the field. "You c'mon to the barn and rest your bones." Some would say Lucy and Sal were nothing but old swaybacked plugs, but they were better than most, and Hank loved them.

He left Lucy and Sal in their stalls feeding on an armload of last summer's wild hay and followed Pa toward the house. Ma or Johanna had struck a light and the cabin looked warm and cheery. It gave Hank courage. He drew his tired, aching shoulders higher. Tonight he was going to ask Pa. Since the morning the new baby came and he ran away, he had worked harder than ever. Maybe Pa would let him have a day all to himself now, to go fishing and poke around the hills? To find the cave-boy again, he thought, but that was a secret he wanted to keep a bit longer.

Hank swallowed his supper fast, then sat squirming on the bench between Johanna and Elsa. If he didn't say something fast his gumption would be gone.

"Pa," Hank blurted suddenly, "tomorrow is Sunday!" Try as he would, he could say no more.

Pa stared at him. "Reckon I know that," he drawled, biting deep into a chunk of cornbread dripping with molasses.

Hank turned hot. He moistened his lips and tried again, "I mean, maybe I could be free tomorrow, Pa, to do a little bass fishin? The breakin' is about done, except for the north slope. I'd sure like a day to just go off and have myself a time—" He studied Pa's face, waiting.

Pa slowly lit his cob pipe. "Call the pigs in first thing in the morning and shell corn to 'em," he said, sucking at the pipe, "and maybe after that you can go." As he moved away from the table, Pa went on, "Want those hogs counted. We'll fatten up the best and in a month or two take 'em to Springfield to sell. Payment is about due on the farm. Don't want to lose the farm."

"I'll have 'em in and counted by first light. Thanks, Pa!" Beaming, Hank elbowed Johanna. "Pass the cornbread. Feel like I ain't had enough to eat. Please." He snatched the molasses pitcher from Clover just as she was about to use it. Seeing the hurt surprise in her sensitive face, he said, "I'll bring you somethin' tomorrow, Sissy, some pretty stones to play with." Sweet Clover, as Mamma called her dark-haired little look-alike, lit up like the morning sun.

"Me, too," Dixie, Clover's twin, said. "I get something, too."

Hank looked across at her. She was messy as usual. Molasses circled her mouth and a bit of sweet potato clung to her square chin. He laughed. "I'm gonna bring you a whole crick to clean up in." Grabbing one of her red-gold pigtails, he used it to wipe the potato off her chin.

Dixie pulled away, sniffed, and plowed her fork into her plate of food. "Last time you went off you near got skinned alive. What'd you do that day you run away, ol' foolish brother?" she asked.

Trouble-making scamp! Hank looked uneasily in Pa's direction. Pa looked thoughtful, but said nothing as the knife in his hand carefully worked at shaping a new axe handle from a chunk of wood. Could it be that Pa didn't think wanting to go out West was such a foolish notion, after all? As he watched the shavings curl and fall, Hank experienced a good, warm feeling toward Pa.

Next day, Hank had trouble finding the desolate cave. His anxiety about wanting to see the cave-boy again made the search seem hopeless indeed.

Chapter Two

At last, Hank recognized a tangle of wild grapevine, then the dark hole. He put his hickory pole and dried gourd containing worms on the ground and lit a torch. As he stood before the treacherous dark of the cave, all the terror Hank had felt that other day inside the cave came washing back over him.

His feet would not move. He started to sweat. The torch flickered in his shaking hand. It was no use. He would have to call the boy out. "H-hoo, friend, are you in there? Like to s-s-see you." Hank cupped a hand behind his ear. His own voice bounced back at him from deep inside the cave, *"H-hoo, friend, are you in there? Like to s-s-see you."*

"Thought maybe you'd like to go fishin' with me," Hank continued, listening for something besides his echo. "Big bass in the deeper pools of that stream yonder."

Might as well admit the truth, he decided. "I'd come in there and t-talk to you b-but this dark old cave has me shinny-shakin' like nothing you ev-ever saw."

Minutes dragged by. Nothing happened. Shucks, why did he think a boy lived in this cave anyhow? Hank asked himself. Made no sense. None of it did. Could it be that getting lost in the cave had addled his brain? He just walked out of that cave, probably, and no wild boy came and saved him.

Hank turned away and rolled his torch in the grass, snuffing out the flame. As he crouched there, a hand came from nowhere and grasped his shoulder. Hank lurched to his feet, his knees threatening not to hold him. "You!" he whispered. "You are real." He watched the other put out his own torch.

For several seconds they stared at one another. Life would be a lot less worrisome, Hank thought, if everybody wore just a scrap or two of cloth and skins. No need to wash...

The cave-boy's glance broke from Hank's and he looked all about.

"I'm alone," Hank said, "if that's concernin' you. Ain't nobody but me." His shaking knees stilled as he saw things about the cave-boy he hadn't noticed the other time.

Under a thatch of dingy yellow hair there was a sort of lonely, scared look in the boy's pale blue eyes. His nose was too big for his face, and ugly, but his crooked grin made Hank think of Clover, and Hank grinned back.

The boy pointed a long, bony finger at Hank's fishing pole.

"Thunderin' toads, yes!" Hank laughed. "I want to go fishing. With *you*. All right? I got extra string and hooks."

The taller boy grinned and nodded.

"C'mon then." Hank snatched up his pole and handed

the other the gourd of worms. He motioned with his arm and struck off for the rushing little stream a few yards north of the cave. "Beats all," Hank said over his shoulder, "how I come to find you. For years I've been hoping to find a friend my age to talk—"

Remembering, Hank felt a bit sick. He turned. "Sorry. Forgot you can't talk." He shrugged. "How'm I going to find out about you? I got more questions in me than in a 'rithmatic book. How can I know your name? I can tell you mine, though; it's Hank. Hank Hedin."

The boy nodded that he understood. He put the gourd on the ground between his long skin-wrapped feet and flung his arm out.

"Yeh, we're going," Hank said, "but not that way. There's a natural good fishin' hole straight ahead." He pointed. "Found it the other time. A nice secrety spot all hid by willows, and pretty."

The other boy frowned and shook his shaggy head. He motioned again in the same direction.

"That's a grove of oaks. Ain't so much as a mudhole over there," Hank exclaimed. The cave-boy poked a thumb into his own chest and again the large hand pointed. Hank began to understand. "Your name? Shucks, I'm stupid! You're tryin' to tell me your name! It ain't oak tree, I hope."

The other's face twisted into a wry grin. He shook his head. Again he patted his chest and pointed.

"Sky," Hank guessed. "Tree—nope. Green? I don't know, but give me a minute, I'll figure it out. You keep pointing at those big oaks."

At that, the cave-boy grabbed Hank by the shoulder and shook him. The nose-dominated face looking down at Hank was wreathed in smiles.

"Oak? No. Oakes? No. Doakes? No. Stokes?" The cave-boy grabbed Hank's and pumped it. Hank threw back his head and laughed. "I figured out your name. It's *Stokes.*" He stopped laughing and watched eagerly as the other made stretching motions between his palms.

"Something more, huh? Tall—so big—" Hank guessed. "Not Bigger, is it? It is!" he exclaimed when the cave-boy nodded triumphantly. "My Pa knew a feller by that name only. 'Twas Bigger Martin."

Hank looked at the other boy for several seconds. "I'll be—" He gently socked the other's arm. *"Bigger Stokes.* Bigger Stokes, talkin' with you is going to be work. But it don't matter," he added quickly, grinning, "it don't matter at all."

The shrug of Bigger Stokes' shoulder plainly agreed. It didn't matter.

∼

LATER, AT THE STREAM, HANK HAULED IN A THRASHING three-pound bass, his fourth fish. Removing the hook from the bucket-like mouth, he said, "Glad your last name wasn't Pierpont, or Wyandotte. We'd never got it straightened out and that's a fact."

Bigger Stokes, on the bank beside him, his feet dangling in the water, nodded and grinned. His white-lashed eyelids were drooping with a contented, drowsy look that made Hank yawn.

"Good day, ain't it?" Hank yawned again, then lay back in the dappled shade beneath the willows, the fish glistening in the grass beside him. The little stream chuckled and gurgled and Hank's drowsy thoughts formed words to the creek's music: "I got me a friend this fine ol' day, I got me a friend."

A short time later, Hank waded into the creek, drank, and splashed the sleepiness from his face. Time to go. The pearly-pink insides of a mussel shell caught his eye and he scooped it from the water. Clover would fuss over it like it was a real pearl and he promised to bring her something.

Hank climbed from the water, drying the shell on his sleeve. He felt, more than saw, that something was wrong. His glance darted to Bigger Stokes and Hank's scalp prickled.

The mute boy's face was crumpled, and his lips quivered as if he was crying, yet no sound came from him. He backed away, staring at the shell in Hank's hand as though it were a sorrowful thing.

Hank looked at the shell and back at his new friend. "Wh-what's wrong?" he whispered. "Ain't nothin' but a little ol' shell. Bigger—Come back, tell me what's so bad about—" He watched, his heart in his throat, not understanding, as the ragged boy tore away, disappearing into green undergrowth.

"It's a shell. Thundering toads, it's just a shell," Hank whispered into the empty afternoon. It was too puzzling.

~

ONE MORNING, A WEEK LATER, HANK TRUDGED TOWARD the barn that clung to the hillside back of the house, his head achy from lying awake most of the night thinking about Bigger Stokes. There had been more than one such night since they had fished together.

Hank shivered in the chill air. It made no sense that

an ordinary little mussel shell would near scare the daylights out of someone. "An' dog take it," Hank hissed aloud, "why's he live by himself, in a cave? Don't he have a ma and pa, somewhere?"

What if he had scared Bigger Stokes so bad he'd never get to see him again? The thought brought an ache of disappointment to Hank's throat. "'I see him again, I'm going to give Bigger one of May's new hound puppies," Hank decided aloud. That would set their friendship back where it ought to be.

Hank forced worry from his mind and moved faster. Pa was at the barn already and his temper would be stirring if he didn't get there quick to help with the chorin'.

He was in mid-step when a thundered oath from the pig pen in the back of the barn set his neck prickling. He started to run, and, lunging through the barn door, saw Pa sagging like an empty tow sack in the back doorway to the pig pen. "What's the matter, Pa?" Hank cried. He rushed to his father's side and looked beyond him.

"The hogs, Pa; what's wrong with them?" Hank gasped. The hogs lay strewn in the spring-fed mud of their wallow, some shivering, backs arched, looking stupid and dull. Most of them, Hank saw a minute later, were already stiff in death.

"Cholera!" Pa said in a voice that seemed to shake the barn. "Cholera on my *farm!*"

"What'll we do, Pa?" Hank croaked. "What do you want me to do? I swear they were all right a week ago. All week they ain't looked like anything like this would happen. I'll help—"

"Can't do nothin'," Pa broke in, his voice hard. "Ain't nothin' we can do now but burn the carcasses and spread lime where they laid. Farm is ruined."

Hank sucked in his breath and ducked as Pa unex-
pectedly smashed his fist into the pole frame of the doorway. "Don't, Pa! Look," he said, unconsciously stepping
away from Pa's anger, "we got the corn seed in the
ground. More'n we ever planted before. Could be we can
get cash money from it. We could still make the farm
payment." Hank motioned with his head toward the
mares asleep in their stalls. "An' we still got the horses.
We can get more hogs, maybe, if we—"

Pa turned on him, his fists doubled, his flaming beard
quivering with anger. "You don't understand, Hank. Hogs
can't be brought onto a farm that's been cholera-hit, not
again for a long, long time. Other stock stand to get it
now too. An' the corn? It won't never do good in this
rocky soil; I've always knowed that."

Seldom had Hank heard Pa's voice so gall-bitter.
Hank turned away from him. "I—I got to feed the
horses and the chickens," he mumbled. "Soon as I've
seen to May and the pups I'll help you b-burn the
hogs."

Looking over his shoulder, Hank saw his father,
broad shoulders drooping, move wooden-like around the
pen of dead hogs, then on up to the top of Baldy Ridge.
Hank's eyes stung when Pa dropped like a sick man to sit
on a rock.

What could he do? Hank tried to shake off his feeling
of numbness and turned his attention to his chores. From
the corner of his eye he saw a shadow fall across the barn
floor from the doorway. It was Elsa, an egg basket on her
arm. She was woolgathering as usual, from the look on
her face.

Hank breathed deeply. "Elsa, tell Mamma we got
trouble. Pa's hogs are all dead, from the cholera. Pa's up

on the ridge an' he—he might be mind-sick, the way he is acting."

Elsa whirled back from the ladder to the loft, her brown braids flying. "What did you say? *Cholera?*" Her blue eyes went wide and the freckles that polka-dotted her broad face seemed to stand out. "That's a terrible disease—Papa's hogs?"

Hank nodded. "Go tell. I'll bring the eggs when I come for breakfast."

For a time after Elsa left, Hank stood motionless. If the farm was ruined, what would happen to them? Outside he could hear the chickens squawking and flapping their wings as Elsa sped by them. In a moment they resumed their happy "ka-kawing." From her stall, Sal nickered softly, then Lucy echoed Sal.

"Comin'," Hank said. "I'm comin', girls." He grabbed the egg basket and took the steps two at a time to the loft. He found seven eggs. Then he pitched a pile of hay over the side for the horses, aiming it carefully so it fell directly in front of their noses.

Outside, Hank threw shelled corn to the chickens. Once, his next chore would have been to milk Greta, the cow. But she was part of last winter's payment on the farm.

Hank took a rabbit down from a rafter where he had hung it after skinning and cleaning it the night before. He hurried to May's box in the far corner of the barn. Hank grinned into the sad brown eyes that looked up at him. "How you doin', girl? How's the young'uns? Brought you a big old jack. Here." May sniffed at the rabbit, then nuzzled her head back into the soft hay of her nest.

"Ain't hungry, huh?" Hank said, patting May's head. He stroked the two brown blobs of fur that were separate and yet part of May. "Take good care of these babies," he murmured. "Some day they'll be the best coon-chasing dogs in Missoura."

It was time for breakfast. Hank went to the back door of the barn, avoided looking at the hogs, and waved at the figure sitting at the top of the ridge. If Pa saw him he made no sign. Shrugging, Hank headed for the house.

"Pa says we're finished," Hank said hollowly, holding his tin plate while Johanna forked four golden pancakes onto it. Johanna's pretty face was white, her violet eyes as clouded with worry as Mamma's.

Mamma, rocking by the stove, pulled the nursing baby closer in her arms. "Papa takes these things powerful hard," she said quietly, "but he comes out of them. You see,"—she spoke as if they were grown men and women seated around the table, or maybe she was talking to herself"August doesn't mind working hard. He just wants it to *pay.* He wants a good life for his family, and he works himself near to death for every gain. Trouble is, when he does get ahead a mite, something— like cholera—comes up to yank the poor man backwards again. This time—" The wrinkle creasing Mamma's forehead deepened.

She said no more, and Hank found himself again wondering what was in store for the Hedins. When he finished eating, Hank hurried back to the barn. Pa was still up on the ridge, he saw. To pass the time, Hank curried the horses. An hour later, Pa still hadn't come down.

He'd better go ahead, Hank decided. He would hitch Lucy up with a singletree, rope the legs of the dead hogs, and have her drag them one by one to a spot a good distance from the barn.

It was a long, disagreeable chore that left Hank covered with cold sweat, his insides churning. Lucy, skittish around the dead animals, had added to the difficulty.

Hank piled brush on the heap and lit it. For a long time the fire crackled and the air was filled with the unbelievable stench of burning hog's hair and diseased flesh.

The fire didn't bring Pa down from the ridge as Hank had thought it might. When the sun was noon-high, he left the smoldering pile and climbed the hill path behind the barn. Reaching the rock where Pa sat, Hank darted a quick look at his father's face. The fierceness had gone out of it. Now Pa's solid, square face looked old and tired and sagging.

"I'm obliged, Son, that you went ahead without me," Pa said.

Hank grinned his relief. After a moment, he said, "Mamma and Johanna ought to have dinner on about now."

Pa pursed his lips, stood up, and put his arm across Hank's shoulders. From the house below came the ringing of the triangle. "They're calling us to eat," Hank said. Pa nodded and sighed. The ringing of the bell echoed from hill to hill, a happy sound, Hank thought, in spite of their troubles.

Except for the clatter and clink of utensils, the noon meal was eaten mostly in silence. It seemed to Hank that Pa was turning something over in his mind, something exciting, possibly, but if so, Pa didn't voice his thoughts.

THAT AFTERNOON, PA AND HANK TOOK THE WAGON down into the valley to the Crossroad Store for lime. Bunker Boxx, the fat little storeman, and Pa talked solemnly for a long while, with much head-shaking.

Then Pa and Hank were on their way home again, Lucy and Sal plodding along the woods road with heads high. Hank smiled to himself. Lucy and Sal were like people. Just now, for instance, they were feeling uppity because they were pulling a wagon instead of dragging a plow.

At home, the lime was spread. "Snow, look at the pretty snow," the twins squealed, coming around the corner of the barn.

"Back to the house!" Pa roared. "It ain't good for you to be out here!"

Hank leaned on his shovel, grinning, watching Clover and Dixie scurry toward the house, darting frightened looks over their shoulders. Most of the time they were Pa's pets, crawling all over him and hugging him near to death. But today Pa wasn't like his usual self.

With the lime-spreading finished, Pa moved determinedly from one uncommon task to another, bidding Hank to help from time to time. Hank itched with curiosity as Pa replaced a broken wagon-wheel spoke with a new one and then, with slow awkward stitching, patched the old canvas wagon cover.

Hank jumped when Pa suddenly ordered him to build a small fire in front of the barn. Soon, Pa was heating and shaping new shoes to Lucy's hooves while Hank held her head, speaking softly into her nervously twitching ear.

Hank could no longer hold the question growing like yeast in his mind. "Pa, are we going somewhere?"

Pa took a long time to answer. "We are goin' *some-*

where, you're right as sunshine in June about that," Pa said finally, emphasizing his words with a ringing tap to Lucy's shoe.

Hank drew in a long, deep breath. "Where, Pa? For how long? Are we moving away from Baldy Ridge for good? How far are we goin'?"

Again, Pa was aggravatingly silent. Hank thought of Bigger Stokes. Leastways, *Pa* could talk, Hank fumed inwardly. So that Pa wouldn't see his angry impatience, Hank lifted his gaze to a black crow winging west across the sky.

Pa must have seen the bird, too. "We're following that bird, Son," he drawled, "just as far west as we can go. Git on, Lucy girl, we're finished with you." Pa slapped the mare's hip and she ambled away, testing her new shoes. "Git Sal," Pa said.

Watching Pa work over Sal, Hank felt exhilaration growing inside him to the point of near-explosion. "You mean it, Pa?" he finally asked, "We really are going—out West?" He searched Pa's face anxiously and saw the answer in his twinkling eyes.

Pa's red beard split into a wide grin. "Leastways I say we are. 'Course it might be we ought to see how the womenfolk feel about it." Pa started to gather his tools and Hank bent to help him.

Hank Henry Hedin, you're going out West! Hank announced incredulously to himself. What he had wanted to do for so long— Cowboy country. Horses, beautiful horses, and lots of them. In the next instant, something seemed to snap inside him. Bigger Stokes, his new friend. He'd never see him again, for sure, if they went away. Confusion made Hank's head swim.

To go out West and to know a boy to be friends with,

those were the two things he wanted more than anything else in the world. One dream seemed to be coming true, but if it did—the other would end. At least his chance of being a pal to Bigger Stokes.

"Pa," Hank said through a dry throat, falling in behind as Pa started for the barn, "I got to tell you somethin'." With quiet urgency, Hank told Pa the strange story of Bigger Stokes, mute cave-boy, his only friend. "Could we take him with us, Pa?" he choked out. "Please? He ain't got a soul in this world but himself, I just know. He's worse off than me. I can't go off and leave him in that cave alone. He's like me, Pa. He needs somebody."

Chapter Three

H ank took a step back on the rocky path to the barn as Pa whirled and faced him. A minute passed; Pa's mouth was set in a tight, perplexed line. "Why are you making up a wild story like that?" he asked finally. "You got a fever, Hank?"

"It's true! All of it's true, Pa. There's a boy can't talk living in a cave a piece from here. I found him the day I —I run off, the day baby Lou Ella was born. I can fetch Bigger Stokes. I can show you he's real, Pa." Hank half-turned, ready to go, but Pa's stern look held him.

"We're talkin' to your Ma," Pa said, "soon as we put away these tools." He shook his head and his heavy brows came unknitted. "Might be she can make sense of what you're saying. First, though, you got to let me break it to her about movin' on."

Mamma looked up as they came through the doorway into the kitchen. Hank could see right away that she knew something was in the air, probably from their faces. She dropped the turnip she was peeling into the bowl in her lap. "What's happened, August?" She stood up, set the bowl on the table, and brushed her dark hair away from her eyes. "Tell me."

Pa did most of the talking, but Hank helped with the part about Bigger Stokes. Hank gnawed at his bottom lip. It was a lot to tell Mamma at one time, he thought. A lot to tell anybody!

When they were finished, Mamma sat down again, and behind her thin fingers pressed against her mouth, she started to smile. Her merry laugh filled the room. "Oh," she cried, "oh, my goodness."

Hank started toward her but Pa got there first. "Nin, honey?" Pa grinned his puzzlement, knelt, and took Mamma's hand in his. "Ninette?"

Her shoulders lifted and dropped in a deep sigh. "So we're going out West?" she said lightly, "and we're taking a-a *cave* boy who can't talk with us? That's what you said?"

Hank and Pa nodded.

"You're both talkin' like you've taken leave of your senses," Mamma giggled. "But if what you're sayin' is so, I'm willin'!"

Hank laughed, relishing the moment as much as Pa, who was hugging Mamma tight in his arms.

It was like Mamma to be ready to go West at the snap of a finger, Hank thought the next morning on his way to Bigger Stokes' cave. According to Pa, Mamma—only fair to middlin' at women's work—couldn't be bested when it came to taking on something new, fun, or adventuresome.

Pa loved to tell that when Mamma was a young girl, her dancing near spun the eyeballs out of folks watching. She was good at telling stories, too, at making sick folk well, and making flowers grow. Hank grinned to himself.

When he left the house this morning, Mamma was digging in the cupboard for her little packets of flower seed while Johanna got ready the more important needs for the westward journey.

This time, finding the cave was not hard. As he neared the shadowy hole in the tangled greenery, Hank's heart pounded. His steps slowed. He wasn't going to stir Bigger Stokes up again if he could help it. The boy acted queer as thunder over the mussel shell.

Hank gulped as Bigger Stokes stepped out of the cave at that instant. The sun's rays caught and dazzled from the blade of a knife Bigger held open in his hand. It was the jackknife he had given him.

"Uh, h'lo," Hank called. He saw the ragged boy dive into the green, lacy underbrush. Hank's throat dried. It was as though Bigger had never been there at all!

"It—it's me, Hank," he ventured huskily. "Don't mean you no harm, Bigger Stokes." He swallowed, and his voice lifted with enthusiasm. "I got somethin' to tell you, Bigger. Something good. C'mon out, please." He waited. "Look, it's me, alone, ol' Hank."

Minutes dragged by, and still, Bigger Stokes did not appear.

Hank tried again. "You might have call to be scared of some folks, but not me. I got one aim only and that's to be your friend. I'm sorry I took you by surprise." Hank sat down in the grass and drew a deep breath. "I'll wait here 'til doomsday if I have to, Bigger, but I ain't leavin' 'til you let me talk somethin' over with you."

Bigger emerged at last, closing the jackknife as he came. He motioned for Hank to follow him out of the open, into dense shrub.

Hank went. Questions about Bigger's caution at

being seen nagged at him. He decided to ask. "I know you can't talk, but with sign language or somethin' can you tell me why you live in the cave yonder? Are you scared of somebody in particular? You run away from your folks?"

Ahead of Hank, Bigger froze, then turned slowly. He smiled, but Hank thought his eyes looked worried. Bigger's shoulders lifted in a careless shrug.

"You mean nothin's wrong?" Hank asked, doubtful. "Honest, now?" He searched Bigger's face. "You live like this 'cause you want to?"

Bigger nodded emphatically, his grin widening.

"You're one of them hermit kind of people don't like to be around other folks, maybe?" Hank said.

Again, the blonde boy nodded.

Hank wasn't convinced, but he decided to get on with what he'd come for. Bigger's past was his own business. Hank found a comfortable spot on a log and, with Bigger squatting on the ground, head cocked, listening, he spilled his dreams of hunting, fishing, and cowboying in the Far West. "What I want is for you to go too, Bigger. Come with us," Hank urged. "Pa and Mamma both say it is all right for you to come."

Hank saw with satisfaction that the mute boy's eyes were shining as he brushed back a matted forelock and stood up. For a body who liked living alone in a cave, Bigger Stokes looked mighty happy at the prospect of going out West with the Hedins, Hank thought.

In the next moment, Bigger's pale blue eyes were boring intently into Hank's. The tall boy's Adam's apple bobbed in his thin neck, desperation distorting his already homely face, as his full, writhing lips struggled to produce sound, and failed.

Compassion stirred in Hank and he could scarcely speak himself. "Don't try so hard," he finally managed. "If you can't talk, it's all right with me." Hank considered for a moment. "I'll do my best to help you learn to talk, though, if you—you *are* comin' with us?"

Bigger Stokes all but danced in his attempt to show how much he wanted to go. With palms up, he signaled Hank to wait where he was and turned alone toward the cave. He returned moments later carrying an animal-skin pouch the size of a man's fist, and a large slingshot.

"That's all?" Hank asked. "Your weapon for gettin' food and your—your whatever that other is, you been gettin' along with just them?"

Bigger tossed off his questions with a shrug. He dropped the pouch inside the neck of his pieced-together shirt, jammed the slingshot inside a strap of leather wound about his waist, and showed with a motion of his arm that he was ready to follow Hank.

Hank couldn't keep from laughing as he led the way. "You're ready to go. I can see that; you're ready!" Still chuckling, Hank broke into a trot. "Near forgot, Pa'll need help with the loading," he said.

As Bigger ran with him, Hank noticed that the other kept a sharp eye on the country—like an eagle, or an Indian. Hank felt a surge of admiration. Livin' alone, wild-like, would sharpen a man's senses that way, he thought. He felt a moment's regret that he had been born and raised in an ordinary cabin.

AT HOME, LATER, HANK PROUDLY TOLD HIS FAMILY AS they spilled into the dooryard, "This is him, my friend,

Bigger Stokes. He said—well, he didn't exactly say it, but he *is* goin' with us." Seeing that Bigger edged toward the open door, Hank added, "Bigger's been living in a cave. Reckon he's anxious to see the inside of a house. Doubt if he has lived regular for a long time. Maybe never. C'mon, Bigger."

In the kitchen, Mamma took Hank aside. "I declare, that boy's filthy!" she whispered into his ear. "He can go, but, mind you, not one step unless he is *clean.* Fetch me the tub and some water to warm on the stove. I'll get the biggest bar of yeller soap I can find. Boy ain't washed in a month of Sundays, you ask me!" Mamma motioned with her head, "He can wash in there in the pantry, so's he'll be private."

"Mamma, he can't talk but he can hear. Anyhow, Bigger ain't so dir—"

Mamma shushed him. "Not so's you would notice. Now get on with what I'm telling you, Son, or take him back to that cave!"

While Bigger bathed, in the backyard Hank stood in the wagon bed receiving folded quilts, kegs holding Mamma's dishes and other whatnots from the girls, and Pa's plow and axe from him. There seemed no end to the line of supplies coming to him.

Hank stowed as much as he could under Pa and Mamma's seat, and under the bench the girls would sit on in the back. He perceived ruefully that he and Bigger would be walking most of the time. But no matter. He would crawl west if that were the only way to get there.

Pa came and nailed a chicken coop to the side of the wagon.

"What happens to the farm after we're gone?" Hank asked.

A stony look came over Pa's face. "Bunker Boxx down at the crossroads store is goin' to buy it. He's comin' this evening to settle up what I've already paid in on the place." Pa's face grew more bitter. "Reckon Bunker thinks that walnut grove will be worth somethin' someday. Could be. As a farm, though, this piece 'a hill is a gut-bustin' failure."

Hank hid his grin. Pa'd never talk so in front of Mamma and the girls. His chest swelled. Pa must consider him nigh a man, equal maybe. Hank went back to work with more fervor. There was a lot yet to do before morning.

The whole family was up at dawn. "Hurry," Hank urged Bigger, who was tackling his ninth syrup-laden pancake. "I had no time yesterday to show you my good ol' hound dog, May, an' her pups. Ain't told you yet, but I'm givin' you one of the puppies."

Hank studied Bigger under lowered eyelids. He was a trifle disappointed in the way the big blonde boy looked. Somehow, it didn't seem natural that he should be clean and wearing Hank's extra overalls and linsey shirt. Another disappointment that rankled him yet was that Bigger had stayed inside all the afternoon before, playing "Puss in the Corner" with the twins.

Even now, Bigger acted like he'd rather stay in the house. Hank sighed. Might be he'd feel the same if he'd not lived in a house for a time. "You just gotta see my dogs, Bigger," he pleaded out loud, and was relieved when Bigger smiled, wiped his chin, and stood up.

In the barn, Hank stood over May's box with his heart in his throat. "It can't be," he thought, over and over again. "It can't be." But it was plainly true. *May was dead.* Through a blur, he watched the whimpering pups nudging the stiffened body of their mother. "P-poor little fellers," he was able to say, finally. Hank reached down for them and passed them up to Bigger's large hands.

Stroking May's velvet ears for the last time, Hank told Bigger in a thick voice, "She was awful old. Old as me. Could be the pups were too much for her, and—she just died quiet. Anyhow, there ain't no signs of the cholera on her. Pa'd not let us take the puppies with us otherwise."

With Bigger's gentle help, Hank buried May beside the house, near Mamma's yellow rosebush. "We got to figure a place for the puppies to ride," Hank told Bigger. They scanned the loaded wagon for a spot. "Here," Hank said. Hanging from the plow handle was the big egg basket. In it were Clover and Dixie's playthings—corncob dolls, stones, and bits of broken dishes.

Hank turned the basket upside down and let the bric-a-brac sift down through the load. A shell fell out, its pearly inside glimmering in the early morning sunshine. It was the one he had given Clover!

Hank's breath caught and he reached quickly for the shell, but Bigger's hand came down over it. Hank tingled all over, awaiting the awful reaction from Bigger. To his surprise, this time Bigger quietly slipped the shell into his pocket, and nothing more. Hank released his indrawn breath. He wanted desperately to ask Bigger what the shell meant to him, but was afraid.

Instead, Hank held up the darker puppy before putting it in the basket. "This is Ullie. For Ulysses S. Grant. Little feller's a natural-born fighter. One you're holdin's named Snoozer. Always sleeping. You pick, Bigger. Which one do you want?"

Bigger pulled Snoozer tighter in his arms and grinned expectantly.

"Sure. He's your puppy now," Hank agreed. "Ouch," he exclaimed, pulling his finger away from the other pup's mouth. "I'll take old fightin' Ulysses. If he don't chew me up, I'll be lucky."

It was time to go. When they heard about May, the twins did not fuss over their scattered toys as Hank knew they would have otherwise. They took their places in the wagon with Elsa and cooed over the pups in the basket. In their coop, the chickens cackled noisily.

Mamma came and climbed to the wagon seat to sit beside Pa, baby Lou Ella in her arms. Hank grinned to himself. Mamma looked like she couldn't wait to go west. Maybe she thought by leaning forward, she could get there faster! He couldn't wait, either—his feet fairly itched to be traveling. Bigger paced, too.

"Pa," Hank blurted, "what's holdin' Johanna?"

"She's sweepin' up," Mamma explained. "Poor, picky-neat girl. She knows as well as I do that nobody's movin' in behind us. But she's got to leave everythin' just so, anyhow."

"Johanna!" Hank bellowed. "We're goin' without you!"

She came running from the house tying her blue sunbonnet under her chin. Glaring at Hank, Johanna said, "You don't have to holler like a sick bull. I'm ready." She climbed onto the wagon seat beside Mamma and carefully arranged her skirts.

"Gonna be an old maid, wait and see," Hank stormed to Bigger.

Bigger's eyes, turned on Johanna, seemed to doubt Hank's words.

Hank snorted and turned his attention to the moment at hand. Pa clicked his tongue, Lucy and Sal threw their shoulders into the harness, and the wheels started to roll. They were on their way out West! Hank's heart thudded with excitement.

At the bottom of the hill, Hank turned for a last look at their old home. He squinted for a better look when something moved in front of the cabin. It looked like a man, he thought, a man in a funny hat—like a stovepipe. But when he continued to watch, there was nothing but the waving branches of the big pine.

Must have been that low branch, Hank decided. Anyhow, if it was a man, it'd just be a scavenger. Some hanger-on from Bunker Boxx's store come to pick over their leavin's. No harm in that, though the feller'd be lucky to find so much as a scrap after Johanna's cleaning!

The road they followed the first three days was little more than a rutted wagon track made worse by the rain that began to fall a few hours after their departure. Still, Lucy and Sal made fair time. They were nigh as anxious to get out West as him, Hank decided with a grin. But they made it hard for him to keep up with the wagon on foot.

Now, on their third night, Hank squirmed deeper into his comforter under the wagon, glad to rest his legs. He opened one eye and viewed the dark lump near him. "S-s-st, Bigger, you awake?"

The lump wiggled in answer.

Hank took a deep breath. "Walk with me tomorrow, Bigger? Mamma'd near give her eyeteeth for a few squirrels to fry. Reckon with that slingshot of yours, we could drop plenty." Hank waited, remembering his disgust when Bigger had squeezed into the wagon with the girls the first day, when Pa put on the wagon cover against the rain.

"Bigger, walkin' we could—" Hank broke off when the dark lump stiffened and lay rigid. "Forget it, Bigger. Go on back to sleep." Hank couldn't keep the disappointment out of his voice. "Ride in the wagon if that's what you want."

The sun stayed out the next few days and the wagon rolled on, down thickly forested hillsides and across narrow valleys. Now and then they passed a farmstead that looked like no more than a tiny quilt patch in the wilderness.

"It's purty," Pa said to Hank one warm afternoon, walking with him while Mamma drove the wagon. "I reckon the Ozark Mountains stand next to heaven for bein' beautiful. But I'm thankful we're leaving. Too many trees, too many rocks for good farming. Bound to be better where we're goin'."

"Where are we headed, Pa? 'Zactly?" Hank lengthened his stride to match Pa's in the rocky road.

"Colorado," Pa said. "Utah territory, maybe. Or California, though it'd take us most of a year to get out that far." Pa grinned. "Tell you what, Hank, when we get to where we're goin', I'll tell you we're there."

Hank failed in his attempt to grin back. Pa's jokes weren't funny when he was dying to know something and Pa made light of it.

After a while, Pa nodded in the direction of the wagon up ahead and said, "That Bigger Stokes likes girl games, or is too lazy to walk, or is scared of somethin'."

"Wish I knew which," Hank mumbled. "Sometimes I get the feelin' Bigger's got somethin' on his mind that worries him awful. When I ask, he acts like there ain't nothin' wrong. As 'tis, he's more Elsa and the twins' friends than mine."

"Likable boy, though," Pa offered. "Ain't no trouble."

"Yeh. Loaned me his slingshot." Hank twisted it out of his pocket to show Pa. "But that's not the same as hunting together." Hank toed a land turtle out of his path, caring not a whit if it snapped his toe off, and plodded on.

Pa shouted for Mamma to stop the wagon; then he hopped on and took over the reins. They came to a good stretch of road and the horses' gait picked up.

IN NO TIME, IT SEEMED TO HANK, HE HAD FALLEN TOO far behind and was running to catch up.

Ahead of him, from inside the wagon, someone screamed.

"What happened?" Hank shouted, racing uphill toward the wagon, which was beginning to slow, finally, as it climbed.

Elsa leaned from the wagon; the twins' heads were framed in the opening beside her. "Puppy!" Elsa screamed, pointing, "Dixie dropped Ullie. Get him, Hank, please!"

He had already spotted the bundle of brown fur rolling down the hill toward him. As Hank ran, he saw the bundle roll to a stop against a rock in the road. There was silence for a few seconds; then Ullie was staggering about, yelping piteously. Hank reached him, grabbed him up, and pulled the puppy close. "You're right fine, little general. No harm done. I got you. C'mon, we got some ground to cover."

The wagon disappeared over the crest of the hill. The

girls' cries were faint from the other side. Hank took a moment to examine the pup, and found him, in truth, to be all right.

A shiver raced up Hank's spine when he realized how alone he was. He set out to follow the wagon, taking a quick look about him. Deep woods lined the road on both sides. His eyes told him he was quite alone, but his pounding heart said differently. He felt that someone, or something, watched him. He looked on either side of the road again, carefully.

When he looked behind him, Hank's breath caught. Slipping out of the brush onto the road about a quarter of a mile behind him was a—a man. A man in a black *stovepipe hat* and black flapping clothes.

For an instant, Hank was too surprised to move. Then he began to run, holding the pup close. He looked back. The man was too far away for him to see his face, but Hank knew he would never forget how the rest of him looked. With his elbows sticking up square, running now, too, garments flapping about him, he looked exactly like a windblown scarecrow come alive.

Hank did not know why he was afraid. He only knew he had never felt such blood-chilling fear as he was feeling this minute. "Pa," he shouted with all his being, "Pa, wait for me!" He reached the top of the hill and started down.

Chapter Four

Hank's breath came in whistles as he ran. Small pains, like slivers of glass, filled his chest. Below him, the wagon wound downhill along the road stretching westward. The team would be stepping lively to keep away from the fast-turning wheels. He'd never catch up!

"Pa," Hank croaked, as loud as he could, "stop. Wait for me, Pa."

Relief flooded him as Pa shouted, "Whoa!" They had heard him, or someone had looked back and seen him running. "Whoa-a-a." The wagon was stopping. Hank chanced to look back. The Scarecrow was nowhere in sight. Still on the other side of the hill, he decided.

Pa left the wagon and came striding back. Hank almost collided with him. "What in tarnation—?" Pa exclaimed, grabbing Hank's shoulders.

Hank hugged the puppy, panted for breath, and couldn't speak. He turned and pointed behind him. "Sc-sc-scarecrow," he was able to say, finally. "Scarecrow chasing m-me. W-watch. He—he'll be comin.' Over the-the hill."

Pa stared at the road for a long time, and then at Hank. His flinty blue eyes rolled skyward and he threw his hands into the air. He glared at Hank then, his face almost as red as his beard. "Yup," he ground out finally, "there's a *scarecrow* a follerin' you. Comin' right down that hill, he is." Pa's voice rose to a roar. "Only one thing wrong. I cain't see no scarecrow!"

Hank shriveled before Pa's anger. "K-keep watchin', Pa," he mumbled, knowing how his story must sound to Pa. "You'll see him. Looks more like a scarecrow than a man. Saw him first as we were leavin' the farm. Then, when I was alone, picking up Ulysses, here, the Scarecrow come chasing down the road after me. 'Bout scared me outta seven years growth."

The anger in Pa's face faded and was replaced by a look of worry. "What's the matter with you, Hank? Look," he said, pointing.

Hank looked back up the hill. It was quiet and peaceful. No scarecrow-like man showed on the dusty road, although heat waves shimmered lazily over the dips. "I saw him, Pa; I did," Hank insisted.

"Twas a mirage," Pa said. "If there's a scarecrow follerin' you, I'll eat him, straw and all! We've lost time enough. Git on the wagon with your mother. Out of the sun, your mind might clear. *Then* we'll talk."

"But, Pa—"

"Git!"

Hank stumbled around the wagon, aware that Bigger and the girls stared open-mouthed. He clambered onto the wagon seat next to Mamma and Pa lunged up after him.

"Giddap!" Pa shouted, slapping the reins. "Hi-yup, git on, Lucy. Sal."

Hank, regaining his breath, was calmed by the soft thud of the horses' hoofs on the road, the creaking harness. Pa'd never listen to him as long as he prattled on like a "'fraidcat young'un." Hank took a deep breath and squared his shoulders.

"Pa," he said quietly, stroking the puppy in his lap, "back home as we were leavin', I did see that sc—that man. Saw him sneakin' in front of the house, behind the big pine. I didn't tell you at the time because first off, I thought I was just imaginin' things. Then I reckoned he was a scavenger, waitin' for us to go, an' I saw no harm in that."

A frown furrowed Pa's brow, but he said nothing.

"Pa," Hank tried again, "do you think he's maybe after our settlin'-up money from the farm? There *is* a feller back there followin' us." He added firmly, "For some reason."

Beside Hank, Mamma spoke, "August, we oughtn't to take any chances. We'd be in a pretty pickle out West with no money."

Pa patted his chest, where deep inside, Hank knew, was the secret vest pocket. "Ain't nobody takin' our settlin'-up money," Pa stated flatly.

"Just the same—" Mamma worried.

"Money's safe, Sugar Face," Pa put an end to the conversation.

After a while, Hank turned to look inside the wagon. "Can you see the sc—anything back on the road, Elsa?" he asked.

She gave a half-look and said disinterestedly, "No. Never did. Don't expect to."

Hank sighed. Nobody cared. The twins were asleep, with Bigger's puppy, Snoozer, dead asleep across their laps. Johanna and Elsa knitted. Bigger lay curled atop a trunk, asleep. Or was he? Hank looked again, sharply. As he watched, a shudder passed over Bigger, shaking his large, bony frame from head to toe.

"Bigger, you sick?" Hank asked, when he saw the shivering continue.

Without opening his eyes, Bigger Stokes nodded and scrunched into a tighter ball.

Mamma was looking too. Her hand found Hank's shoulder. "The poor boy," she whispered. "Looks like he's comin' down with something. I'll fix him some yarb tea when we stop. Might be the ague. Or could be he's just homesick—though heaven only knows for what."

Some of the worry inside Hank let go, and he began to relax. Mamma would take care of Bigger. With her lookin' out for him, nothin' very bad could happen. It was plain he'd be the only one worryin' about the Scarecrow.

Hank asked Elsa and Johanna again to look and see if someone followed. He had asked so often that they now pretended not to hear him. The Scarecrow is back there somewhere, Hank told himself, wondering if his mind might have played tricks on him. No, he decided. He'd seen him.

Around them, the countryside was changing, the hills beginning to flatten somewhat. Trees were fewer, Hank noticed. Velvety-fine green grass waved in a warm wind. Beside him, Pa was sitting up straight, his eyes aglow.

"We've seen about the last of Missoura," Pa announced with satisfaction. "That's Kansas prairie ahead of us, sure!"

Itching to have his own look-see down the road

behind them, and to explore, Hank passed Ulysses to Elsa and asked to be let off the wagon. "I'll get some supper," he said, pulling the slingshot from his pocket.

Hank studied the rolling green terrain behind them, long and hard. There was no sign of the weird, flapping, scarecrow-like creature. He must have given up, he decided, whatever he was after them for.

Soon after, Hank spotted a rabbit, frozen like a statue, on a knoll before him. He took a stone from his pocket, armed the slingshot, and lifted it to eye level. When the sinew was stretched taut and the rabbit sighted carefully in the crotch, he let fly.

"Rabbit stew!" Mamma said happily, when he handed the big jack up to her on the wagon. "Our boy won't be sick for long, now."

Hank circled the wagon to where he could look in at the big, blonde boy asleep on the trunk. His friend looked to need curing, sure enough.

He was glad when, an hour later, Pa headed the wagon off the road toward a wild plum thicket. Walking beside the wagon, knee-deep in grassy weeds from last year, Hank could hear the excited cries coming from within. "We're stoppin'! Gonna make camp." And from fat little Dixie, "I'm so hungry my stomach is cryin'!"

Beyond the thicket, Hank found a gully, cut deep, zigzagging across the prairie. Except for a few small pools mirroring the red setting sun, the creek was dry. Hank shrugged. He would have liked to swim. They were lucky, though, to have water for cooking.

"It's so nice here," Mamma crooned as she bustled about. Her glance followed a meadowlark flashing from branch to branch in the thicket. "Could we stay, August? A day or two? It'd do the Stokes boy good. I could get the baby's things washed out and dried." She rummaged through the food box. "Tomorrow I could cook us a big pot of beans, and Johanna could make biscuits."

Pa laughed and planted a kiss on her cheek. "I reckon we could do that. We been on the road a week. We'll have us a rest. Get the boy well."

"What do you s'pose is wrong with him, Pa?" Hank questioned as they made his friend comfortable on a pallet near the campfire. With dread, he remembered that Bigger hadn't bothered to open his eyes, even, as they moved him. "He's shiverin' terrible but it ain't cold. Will he—he be all right?"

"Looks kinda like malaria," Pa mused. "Saw it down South during the war. But I dunno. It's not altogether the same, either. It's like the boy's took himself out of this world into his own. Beats me. But Mamma can fix him if it can be done at all."

Hank knew it was true but couldn't help worrying a little. At last, after supper, weariness swept all worries from Hank's mind, and he fell asleep almost before he could crawl into his blankets.

Next morning, Bigger seemed better. In the shadow of the wagon, Hank helped him eat. "Don't quit 'til it's gone," he urged, holding the bowl of cornmeal mush steady for his friend. "We gotta get you over this spell of sickness. We're spendin' a couple days here. We could explore. Look for arrowheads. I aim to search the gully yonder to see if any of it is deep enough for fishin'."

Bigger rolled back onto his pallet, turned his thin gray face away, and closed his eyes. Hank's shoulders fell. "All right," he sighed. "We'll do those things when you're ready." Pa was right. It seemed as if Bigger was far, far away in some other place and did not know that he, Hank, was right beside him.

Feeling grim, Hank turned to his chores. He carried water for Mamma, curried the horses, and helped Pa grease the wagon wheels. Every few moments he looked at Bigger. The boy still shivered. At times, it looked as though his light blanket would dance off him and Hank would leave his work and tuck it back in place.

If anything happened to Bigger Stokes, Hank thought unhappily, it would be his fault. He had talked Bigger into leaving Missoura. What if Bigger was livin' alone, wild-like, in a cave? At least he wasn't ailin' then.

In the afternoon, Hank stretched out on the ground near Bigger, planning to rest for a few minutes. He awoke with a start sometime later, thinking it was the middle of the night. Looking quickly about him, he saw heavy storm clouds being blown across the sky. It was still day. Mamma and Johanna were snatching clothes from the thicket branches where they had hung them to dry.

Hank yawned, got to his feet, and studied the sky. He might get a little fishing done, providing he could find a deep enough hole before the rain came. Evening was perfect for catching catfish. He looked down at Bigger and again felt a twinge of disappointment. Bigger didn't look so gray as before, but neither did he look fit to go fishing.

After traveling the gully's edge north for some distance, Hank at last came upon a liberal stretch of water. He baited the hook with one of a half-dozen grasshoppers he had caught on the way. "C'mon, you ol' bait stealers," he whispered, "I'm sick of mush for breakfast. I want me some catfish, fried crisp and brown."

Almost immediately, he caught two catfish, but the next half-hour passed without a nibble. Hank pulled in his line, threaded his catch on a forked stick, and moved on up the bank.

He tried a second spot, without luck. Continuing on, Hank saw that the gully made a sudden, zigzagging bend back eastward. He hesitated. Mamma'd have supper cooked soon. Still, two fish weren't enough for breakfast, even for him alone. He would give it one last try.

Around the next turn a flash of movement caught Hank's eye. He stopped. His heart pounded furiously. His throat dried.

Several yards ahead at the bottom of the gully, the Scarecrow squatted beside a pool! The man gave a short turn toward the campfire he was lighting, and Hank caught a glimpse of a hawkish face and long, black hair.

Stooping, with one cautious step after another, Hank backed away from the gully. Then he turned and raced for camp. They never should have stopped for a day's rest! The Scarecrow had caught up!

Coming in sight of his family grouped around the campfire, Hank slowed to a walk. No use running in screaming, Hank knew. Pad only think him a cockeyed fool again. Still, it was all Hank could do to hold his voice down from a shout. "Pa," he said hurrying to his father's side, "I saw him again. The Scarecrow. I can prove it this time. Look there. See that smoke 'way off there? That's his fire!"

A drop of rain spattered on Hank's cheek as he waited.

Pa rose from where he had been squatting in front of Bigger and handed Mamma a plate of food. "See what you can do," he said. "I got him to eat part of a biscuit."

Pa's eyes narrowed as they took in the smoke lifting into the sky in the east. After a moment, he nodded.

"I was right, wasn't I, Pa!" Hank exclaimed, his heart thundering with excitement. "That Scarecrow feller is after us and he ain't give up!"

When Pa spoke, Hank could scarcely believe his ears.

"Nope," Pa said, "you ain't necessarily *right*. So a feller is over yonder cooking his supper? That gonna do us harm? What proof have you got that he's *after* us? Hank, there ain't no law against his traveling the same direction we are. Moving West is an idea common to a lot of folks."

"But, Pa," Hank protested, "he was sneakin' around our place back at Baldy Ridge just as we were leavin'!"

"Didn't say he wasn't," Pa's voice was aggravatingly calm. "Like you said, he could be a scavenger. Saw us pulling out and wanted to see if we left anythin'. Maybe he was hungry. Thunderation, the man could just be travelin' the same road we are."

Hank started to interrupt again but Pa stopped him.

"Wait now," Pa said. "He might have the notion to rob us. I don't discount your idea entirely. To make sure that don't happen, you and me are going to take turns standin' guard. We'll be wastin' our time like as not." A slow grin spread across Pa's face. "We got to do somethin'," he mimicked, "otherwise you an' your ma will have us killed in our beds, the way you're talkin'."

Hank grinned. It was enough. Pa'd find out he was right. But he didn't say so, aloud.

Pa gave Hank the first watch after helping Bigger into the wagon. The rest of the family lay rolled in their blankets in a shelter Pa had improvised under the tangled thicket, out of the way of the coming rain.

The first sharp crack of thunder made Hank want to run and hide, but he threw his shoulders back and continued pacing the outer edge of camp. Above him, serpent tongues of lightning rent the night sky again and again, each time followed by rolling thunder. Then the cold, wet rain sluiced down. Hank scrunched deeper into his collar, shoved his hands in his pockets, and paced. He stubbornly pushed thought of warm blankets from his mind. Any minute the Scarecrow could jump him, he thought. His glance darted around, trying to penetrate the dark. The rain wouldn't stop a feller so determined as the Scarecrow looked to be.

TWO MISERABLE HOURS PASSED WITHOUT INCIDENT; THEN Pa came to relieve him. Hank raced for the shelter and his blankets, more than glad to have Pa take over the rest of the night's watch.

Hank was awakened next morning by the high-pitched voices of his sisters quarreling over breakfast chores. Girls, he thought in disgust. They ought never to have been created. He groaned, the sound long and ugly even to his own ears, and staggered from his damp bed. Outside the thicket the sun dazzled. He became aware of a strange roar.

Moving toward the gully to wash in a puddle, Hank stopped short. The gully, which only last night had been nearly empty, was full to the banks!

Hank stared at the swift brown water, shocked. A tree, newly budded, swung by on a crest as he watched. The roaring—it was this—river, which had happened overnight—a gully washer!

Shaking his head, Hank slogged back through the mud to the fire. Pa was waiting for him.

"I decided we ought to talk to that stranger," Pa announced. "We'll get that over and done. Can't head out, no way, until this water goes down. Eat your breakfast. Then we'll go."

Hank started to answer, then swallowed hard as realization hit. "P-p-pa," he stammered. "Th-that Scarecrow, that f-feller was c-camped down in the g-gully. Down in the bottom of the gully."

Pa stared at him and said something under his breath. "Are you sure, Hank?" he asked after a moment.

Hank nodded. "He was. Had his fire down there."

Pa shook his head, his lips tight. "Gully washer—a flash flood like this—if he was asleep down there it could of took him unawares. He'd never know—" Pa's voice trailed off and he stroked his beard.

"We'd better look for him, right, Pa?" Hank asked. "I can eat when we get back."

They searched an hour, then Hank saw the hat. He ran forward and lifted it with a shaking hand from where it was caught in a bush by the stream. "It's his," he mumbled. "He was wearing this old stovepipe hat."

Pa frowned. "We'll never rightly know what it was he was after, if anythin'. Ain't no use lookin' for his—body. It'll be a far piece from here."

Hank walked close beside Pa as they headed back to camp.

The family listened, saying nothing, with shocked surprise on their faces. Then Hank saw Bigger leaning, white-faced, from the back of the wagon. "Wh-what's the matter, Bigger?" Hank asked. "What do you want? What are you d—"

Bigger dropped down out of the wagon and stumbled to Hank. He snatched the hat from Hank and threw it on the ground.

The family knotted together, watching, as Bigger lurched and staggered, trampling the hat deeper and deeper into the mud.

Mamma was the first to move. "It must be the fever. Poor boy's out of his head. August, Hank, help me get him back to bed."

Hank rushed forward and gripped Bigger's arm. "You —you durn sick fool," he said huskily, his voice catching. "What'd you do that for?" He looked into the pale blue eyes but there was no answer there, only pain.

Chapter Five

After the incident of the flash flood, Bigger quickly improved. Whether he got better because of Mamma's hovering over him, or something else, Hank couldn't be sure. Whenever he brought up the subject of Bigger's sickness, his queer behavior with the hat, Bigger's eyes would plead for him not to talk about it, or he would grow angry and walk away. Hank decided to forget it, for a while.

He was happy to have Bigger walking with him now, and Hank wished they might swing south into Indian Territory. There would be excitement aplenty down there for boys hankering for adventure, he told himself.

Instead, Pa urged Lucy and Sal north along the Neosho river, deeper into Kansas. One morning, after breakfast, Hank and Bigger started to load bedrolls and cooking pots into the wagon in readiness for the day's journey on through Council Grove Valley.

"Stop," Pa spoke up suddenly. "Leave things as they be."

"Why?" Hank questioned, turning. There was a

strange smile on his father's face, and Pa paced back and forth, his flaming beard lifted high.

"Why, Pa?"

"This is it!" Pa announced. "We're camping on this here spot until I can get us a farm!"

"In Kansas?" Hank protested. Before he could stop himself, Hank was shouting, "Pa, Kansas ain't out West!" With effort, he was able to lower his voice. "It's only April, Pa," he pleaded. "We got *all summer* for traveling." Pa didn't even seem to hear. Hank listened, feeling sick, to Pa's joyful laugh.

"April's plantin' weather!" Pa boomed. "I never saw such land right for plowin' and plantin'." He strutted away from them, out into the open, away from the dwarf willows and cottonwoods that bordered the stream where they camped. He gazed about as though Kansas were one huge green pie he could feast on the rest of his days.

Muttering some pet words of Pa's, Hank left Bigger leaning against the wagon and went to meet Mamma and the girls hurrying up from the river, where they had been tidying themselves. Making no attempt to hide how he felt, Hank told them of Pa's decision, hoping for something but not knowing what.

"Now, Hank," Mamma chided as she plaited her brown hair, "August knows what's best for us. If we're homesteading in Kansas, so be it."

Hank's angry glance followed Mamma, who settled herself on a keg beside the dying breakfast fire, a basket of quilt scraps in her lap. She threaded a needle, then held it between her teeth while she searched and selected first one bright scrap, then another. Now and then she looked toward Pa with a twinkle in her eye, shaking her head.

Hank felt he couldn't breathe. He whirled toward the

girls and saw that they were setting up housekeeping in the "rooms" formed by the branches of a fallen cottonwood. The baby's basket was hooked over a low limb and there little Lou Ella cooed and swang. As they tried to keep up with the girls, the puppies, Ullie and Snoozer, bounced and rolled.

Hank's eyes burned. "Women!" he hissed. "Farmin'! It ain't fair!" He strode from camp toward the open prairie. When he realized Bigger was close behind, Hank slowed, and for a long time they walked, the wind-riffled bluestem grass like velvet underfoot.

They came to a large, cup-like bed of bluish-gray shale and here Hank slumped to rest. Inside he felt as hollow and pithy as a dead tree. "I shoulda took that freight train long time ago," he told Bigger, hunkering beside him. "If I get stuck on a *farm* I'll never get to be a cowboy."

Bigger's eyes were sympathetic. His big hand rested lightly on Hank's shoulder.

"Maybe Pa won't be able to find a farm," Hank told Bigger hopefully as they made a wide circle back to camp. "Might be all this belongs to somebody else and the only land left for settlin' is further west."

Bigger stroked his large nose in thought and nodded. His eyes began to shine with devilment. He motioned Hank to watch. He touched Hank's arm, then himself. With his hands before him as though clutching reins, Bigger trotted away on an imaginary horse, his bony knees swinging high.

Hank laughed and ran to catch up. "We'd have us a time, wouldn't we?" he said breathlessly to Bigger, who was now a boy again—walking. "Our own ponies. Ridin' the range. Herdin' cattle. Just moseyin' around the country when we didn't feel like workin'. All them places," he said, a wistful yearning in his chest. "The Montana country, Wyoming, TEXAS! I heard talk about 'em down to Bunker Boxx's store. If Pa don't get a farm —" Hank's throat filled and he could say no more.

Back at camp, Hank shuffled to the far edge and sat on the ground. Bigger dropped beside him. Pa squatted beside Mamma, counting and recounting the settling-up money from the Missouri farm. Although he pretended to pay no attention, Hank was aware of Pa's every move.

After several minutes, Pa put away the money and got to his feet. He pounded the dust from his battered felt hat against his knee, pulled the hat on, hard, and swiped a balled fist across the toe of each worn boot. Without turning to look at Hank, he said, "Son, you're in charge while I'm gone. Don't let nothin' happen to our girls."

Hank choked back words that might get him into trouble and nodded. He had no right to wish failure on Pa, but...He watched Pa ride away across the prairie. He wanted to shout, "Pa, you promised, you promised we'd go out West." But he held his tongue. Anger toward Pa created an ugly feeling inside him. He didn't like the feeling.

THREE NIGHTS LATER, HANK WATCHED PA RIDE BACK into the circle of light from their campfire. Pa sat Lucy high and sassy-like. It was done. Pa had a farm. It was easy to see that. Inside, Hank could feel his bitterness slipping away. Pa looked so happy. Hank grinned to himself, relieved because he could at least feel glad for Pa.

Between mouthfuls of hominy and fried rabbit, August Hedin eagerly described their new home. "Sixty acres, not raw prairie; it's been tilled a few years. It's a day from here. No fences yet, but we'll plant hedges of osage orange." He looked at Mama and announced proudly, "You won't have to wait for us to build a house, Ninette. Little stone house already there, built by the fella who homesteaded the place first. Sod barn, too. We got us a fair creek—" Pa hesitated and reddened, "a—mile from the house. We'll dig us a well 'soon as we can, Nin," he finished quickly.

Hank, squatting beside Pa, wasn't ready for the sudden clap of his father's hand on his knee and almost fell over.

"No stump-grubbin' for you no more, Hank," Pa said. "We got deep rich soil to work."

Hank gripped his plate of food to keep from losing it as Pa gave his knee a firm shake. "With you boys' help we can make this farm pay off. Them tobaccy plantations in Missoura won't be no high shakes to the farm we're goin' to have!"

Looking up at Bigger, Hank saw his friend shrug helplessly.

Still, a day later when he and Bigger followed Pa about their new farm, Hank couldn't help feeling a rise of interest, particularly when he compared it to the hilly, stone- and stump-ridden acres at Baldy Ridge.

First, Pa took them to the limestone quarry located in the far corner of the south forty. "You boys can bring rocks from here to build pig and sheep pens behind the barn," Pa said. "All this'll be wheat ground," he said, including in his sweeping arms the grassy land from where they stood to the little stone house.

As they walked past the house, Pa mused, "Not enough trees. Just the big elm in front and the mulberry back of the house. Mamma wants an orchard and a garden. Got to git a well in." He waved at the twins playing house under the mulberry tree.

"This road goes on north to a town called Pillar," Pa said, as they continued their tour along the property line. "We got no close neighbors now, but there's an old empty shack just north of our place. Maybe some folks'll move in." Pa's booted feet came down hard as though his toes wanted to reach through the soles and feel the earth. "This'll be corn here. Maybe broomcorn yonder. There's a railhead at Skiddy, if we get to farmin' big and want to ship our crops."

Pa talked so proud, so sure. Bigger and me would feel like that, Hank thought to himself, a trace of resentment returning, if we were out West doin' what we want.

They had reached the far north corner of their land and Pa stood, frowning. "Look yonder," he said, "see them white-bloomin' weeds along that ridge? Jimson. Poison to stock. I'd git rid of them if they was on our land. Might anyway."

As they crossed the boundary line and walked on, Hank thought the ridge looked like a giant's arm, knotty with muscle, flung across the prairie. The shoulder sprang up just beyond their boundary, and the crumpled fingers lay some distance north past the abandoned soddy. Jimson Ridge. Jimson Ridge was a giant's arm. The shack was an earthen lump in the crook of the arm, and had one window, one door, and a chimney.

Pa stopped when they reached the soddy. He stood, thoughtful, his hands in his pockets. The wind picked up and whistled around the empty shack. A dry weed skipped across the barren dooryard.

The eerie whine of the wind sent a sudden and unexpected shiver racing up Hank's back. He looked at Bigger and saw from his frown and the set of his full lips that he too felt strange.

"Better git back," Pa said solemnly.

Hank and Bigger fell into step behind him.

They were nearing the house when Pa cleared his throat, breaking the silence. "I know this ain't cowboy country to your mind, Hank. But you'll come to like it just the same. And it ain't all farmin'. Up in the Smoky Hill country there's a bunch of horses runnin' just as wild and free as you please. What do you think of that? Heard about them horses in Pillar, the day I was in to ask about farms for sale. *Wild* horses. Right here in Kansas."

Pa waved his arm. "Cattle-drivin' trails are all around us. They bring herds of cattle up from Texas on the Chisholm Trail, the Shawnee Trails. Kansas is more out West than you boys know!"

Pleasure and shame mingled inside Hank. Pa cared a lot how he felt! Hank looked at Bigger and felt himself beaming. Could be they would like it here. Pa *wanted* them to like Kansas. "Don't you wish we could go catch us a couple of them wild horses?" he whispered aloud to Bigger.

But instead of growing to like the Kansas farm, Hank hated it more and more as one long day of hard work followed another. Limestone, soft and easy to cut when dug, was hard by the time they had hauled, heaved, and thumped it into place to make pens behind the barn.

Inside the sod barn, one end was sectioned off, and

here Hank used precious crates to build a row of nests for Mamma's laying hens.

Large patches of ground were plowed and planted to corn and spring wheat.

Every job, it seemed to Hank, was interrupted by somebody hollering *water*. It was needed constantly—for washing clothes and cooking, for watering the newly-planted cottonwood windbreak and the corn and wheat, now green rows in the black soil. The novelty of hauling water in barrels by wagon soon wore off and Hank hated no chore more than the never-ending trips to the creek.

The one real pleasure, he decided, was heading for the house each nightfall! Before he got anywhere near the door, Hank could smell Mamma's flowers that had done away with the ugliness of the little stone house. Morning glories framed the two front windows and flower beds under each window in back held a sweet-smelling mass of petunias, bachelor buttons, and spicy pinks. Used dishwater and clotheswater kept them green and blooming.

Inside the house colorful rag rugs dotted the floors. On a shelf above the fireplace were Pa's three books from the old country, printed in Swedish and, for Hank, unreadable. By the books was Mamma's china vase with a pink moss rose blooming on its fat curved side.

The best part of going to the house was getting to ease his weary, aching body into bed after supper by lamplight. Usually Hank was too tired to talk to Bigger on the cot next to his. "Ain't got no more need of a tongue than Bigger does," Hank thought to himself one night.

The thought occurred to Hank again the next morning as he hoed corn under a blazing sun. "You know," he said to Bigger, who was hoeing the row next to his, "I'm so plumb wore out most of the time I'm turning into a hand-waver and eye-blinker just like you. Too tired to talk. I wish," Hank said, "Pa had let us go with him into Pillar today, instead of taking all the girls and leaving us home to work. Ain't fair," he ground out.

If Bigger heard, and Hank was sure he had, the big blonde boy gave no sign. "Bigger!" Hank snapped, "are you listening? Thunderin' toads, I wish you could answer me, talk back to me. Ain't you never knowed how to talk?"

Slowly, Bigger turned. Under the hot sun Hank waited. Finally, Bigger nodded—just barely.

Hank's breath caught in surprise. "You did! But why'd you quit? What happened? I just always figured—Bigger, how come you can't talk now if you once did?"

"What happened...?" Hank began again. He broke off when he saw the terror creeping into Bigger's pale eyes, glazing them over. Chills raced up his own spine at the sight. Hank reached out a hand.

Suddenly, Bigger whirled away, running.

"Wait!" Hank dropped his hoe and ran after him. "Bigger. You can tell me. We can talk, you with your hands and eyes and all. You *could* tell me. Everything—"

He caught up and grabbed Bigger's shoulder. Bigger struck his arm down with a blow that sent pain rocketing through Hank's whole arm. "Durn you!" Hank cried. "You don't have to hit me. I was trying to help—" He dove for Bigger's fleeing legs and brought him to the ground, hard.

Hank threw himself astraddle Bigger's back and out of desperation managed to hold the larger boy pinned to the ground until Bigger's furious struggling ceased. "H-had en-enough?" Hank panted finally, his own anger and hurt fading.

Bigger turned his face sideways and glared up at him. He stuck out an unusually long rosy tongue that picked up dirt before he drew it back. Hank couldn't hold back the laugh that welled up inside him. He rolled away from Bigger, laughing hysterically, clutching his middle with his arms. "Whew!" he gasped, opening his eyes at last.

Bigger stood over him, staring, his face beet-red.

Hank stopped laughing. "Bigger," he said quietly, "I don't give two hoots in a holler about whatever's happened to you before, how you come to live wild in a cave, if you don't want to tell me. Ain't askin' ever again." Hank sat up and drew his overalled knees to his chest. "What's the harm in tryin' to learn to talk again, though, an' me helpin' you?"

Seconds ticked by, then Bigger grinned crookedly. His lips worked but no sound came out.

Hank caught Bigger's large wrist and pulled him to the ground. "Wait, now—like this," Hank said patiently. "Say 'Hank.' 'Hank.' Open your mouth wide, like this, then bring it shut quick, like—like you was chompin' an apple." Again and again Hank said his name, showing his friend.

Bigger tried, working his mouth exactly like Hank's, open—shut, open—shut, until Hank could almost hear Bigger saying his name, though there was no actual sound coming from Bigger's sun-scorched lips.

As usual, Hank felt sad watching the uncommon, desperate struggle to speak. He clapped Bigger's knee. "Don't quit," he said huskily. "Keep tryin' to say my name, all the time. I—I ain't never cared 'til now, but I got to hear you say it. Sometime. I want you to say my name."

Hank and Bigger turned in the same instant toward the faint but growing sound of creaking wheels and muffled girl voices on the road. Hank got to his feet. "They're back. Let's go meet 'em."

In the yard, Hank stared at the yellow cow tugging on the rope that tied her to the rear of the wagon, at her single, twisted horn. Mean, he decided instantly. An ornery cow if he ever saw one. Up in the wagon bed the girls were united in holding down a squealing black pig.

Elsa, red-faced and sweating, spoke wearily. "The cow's name is Jezebel. The old dev—" she darted a frightened look at Pa and covered her mouth.

Dixie was braver. "The old devil gave us trouble all the way home," she said matter-of-factly, dropping down out of the wagon.

"Give the girls a hand," Pa roared, moving Hank and Bigger into sudden action. "Put up our new critters. I got the doubtful pleasure of breakin' the news to your ma that we ain't got a dime left in this world." Grinning nervously, Pa gathered up an armload of bundles and headed for the stone house.

Jezebel fought and bellowed all the way to the barn. Inside, Hank tied her in a stall, rubbed his aching arms, and went to give Bigger a hand with the pig.

The twins were soothing her in her pen with turnips from Mamma's garden. To Hank's disgust, the little girls were calling the grunting, filthy creature, "Lady Beth."

Hank and Bigger went back to the barn. Hank could scarcely see the cow through a cloud of dust. "Why-why y-you—!" Hank sputtered. "I see it," he answered Bigger, who pointed at a hole in the side of the barn. "Big enough to crawl through." Brilliant sunrays filtered through the dust. "She got her no-good backside around there on purpose, just so she could kick thunder out of the barn wall!"

Jezebel rolled her eyes sideways at them and gave her whole body to a long, low bellow that seemed to shake the small barn.

"Listen. Thinks she's one of them wild Texas longho —" Hank started to say. He broke off as an idea came to him. He turned to Bigger. "You know what we got here?" he asked gleefully, almost choking on his words. "We got us a *wild critter.* We can learn cowboyin' with this old she-devil!"

Bigger drew his head back, questioningly, and Hank knew immediately what the other boy was thinking. "No, Bigger! Pa wouldn't mind. He'd want us to tame her. Besides, I'm sick of all work and no good times."

Bigger shrugged, still looking doubtful.

" 'Member that old hide rope we found when we moved here? It's near wore out but we can fix it. Where'd we put it?" Hank started to look, but Bigger was already taking the coiled lariat from a peg on the wall behind them.

"Cowboys call 'em their catch rope," Hank explained, reaching for the rope. "You tie a sort of eye in the end like this, so the rest of the rope can go through it and make you a loop. They swing the loop 'round over their heads," Hank continued, leading the way out of the barn, "then throw it right down over the cow's or horse's head, and *yank.*"

Hank stopped and pointed at Mama's red rooster pecking away at a mulberry on the ground.

Bigger nodded and grinned his crooked grin.

Hank twirled the rope over his head, controlling the circle. He let the noose sail out and drop. "We'll have to work at it a mite," he said, embarrassed, dragging in the rope. The noose had fallen so far short of the rooster that it continued to peck away at the mulberry unconcerned.

"You try it," Hank said, giving the rope to Bigger. "But don't feel bad if you miss. Catchin' and bustin' ol' Jezebel will be easier."

It was easier to rope the cow. It was easy, too, to rope Johanna, Elsa, and the twins. When they were finally able to snag Ulysses S. Grant and Snoozer on the run, Hank knew he and Bigger were probably as good as any two cowhands in the West.

Why did they have to be stuck on a little ol' Kansas farm, anyhow? Hank asked himself time after time.

∼

HE STILL DID NOT HAVE THE ANSWER WHEN MIDSUMMER came and the new farm started to die before their eyes. Under the scorching sun, the grass died, the creek dried to cracked clay, the corn—like bacon in a hot skillet— frizzled and turned brown before ears could form. Seeing it, Hank was secretly glad. Now they'd probably go on out West.

Chapter Six

"What are we going to do?" Hank asked. He came up beside Pa, who stood with slumped shoulders, staring at his dead corn patch.

"Do?" Pa booted a cornstalk out of the dry dust. "Haul water. There's a feller and his wife live eight miles or so east of here that has a well. I reckon they'll let us have water. We'll just be hauling it a little farther."

"I thought—"

"You thought we'd pull up and move on again," Pa finished for Hank. "Nope. This is a good farm. We just need water. Some way or other I got to dig a well, and git us a windmill."

"What about vittles, Pa?" Hank insisted. "We've got nothin' to eat hardly. The supplies you got in Pillar are gone."

"We won't starve." Pa's chin jutted out. "We've got potatoes and turnips that Mamma growed. Flour and sugar is for fancy folk, anyway."

More rabbit stew, Hank thought disgustedly. They

had been living on it for so long he was surprised the whole family didn't hop around like rabbits. Suddenly, Hank was aware that Pa had put a question to him, a strange question. "What did you say, Pa?"

"I said," Pa drawled, an edge to his voice, "what do you think of looking for work in Pillar?"

"Me!" Hank was astonished. "Work? I don't know how to work—do town work, I mean."

Pa looked close to losing his patience. "Hank, the drought's been hard on most of the farmers, so there ain't no use in your looking for farm work. I'm thinkin' of a store job. If you could get us some cash money we could buy more seed. I'd stay here and get the well dug. Might be I can buy a windmill on credit, with promise to pay from my first good crop. I could throw in that Jezebel cow—hadn't ought to of bought her so soon, anyway."

Caught up in thought, Hank didn't reply right away. What would it be like, getting a job, living away from the folks, in town? Might be a cow outfit would pass through, and...Aloud, he said, "Bigger, too. With both of us workin' there'd be twice the cash money."

Pa shook his head. "Ain't a good idea. Two of you lookin' for work would just halve your chances. An' Bigger—well, it has to be you because Bigger can't talk. That might be held against him. Bigger can help me, though, gittin' the fields ready again."

It was plain that Pa's mind was set. "When do I go, Pa?"

"Tomorrow," Pa told him, kindlier. "Better git off before first light."

Hank nodded and slowly turned away. "I got to find Bigger and tell him."

He found him in the barn splicing their rawhide rope

with pieces from an old boot. When Hank told him he had to go to Pillar to try to find work, a hint of a frown crossed Bigger's face; then he grinned. To Hank's surprise, Bigger's rough hand caught his hand and shook it. He tried to say "Hank."

"That's—that's right, keep tryin'," Hank said. "Keep workin' at sayin' my name while I'm gone." He pulled his hand free, afraid of the feeling coming over him. "It ain't like I was going far," he said stoutly. "Like—like out West, or somethin', without you. I'll be comin' home for visits, every chance I get. You—you take care of yourself an' take care of Mamma, an' Pa. An' don't let them fool girls drive you loco."

By the time Hank strode into Pillar the next day, the sun was riding high in a cloudless blue sky. He didn't know how the town got its name, but he could guess. In the center of town stood a huge, umbrella-like elm, the biggest tree he had ever seen. All along the main street, dusty, false-front buildings leaned toward the giant elm as though for support.

Here and there between the stores, wispy cotton-woods and honey locusts grew like skinny second cousins. Hank hurried, excitement building inside him. Overhead, dry leaves rustled in the hot wind. From a blacksmith shop far down the street came the clear, bell-like ring of hammer against anvil.

Hank juggled his sack of belongings to a more comfortable position over his shoulder and, running a hand back over his sandy-red hair, eyed the old men on a bench in front of the general store. It was shady there, and most of the men were dozing. He would like to rest, too, for just a mite, but he had more important things to do, Hank told himself.

Entering the store below a sign that said McCRACK-EN'S, Hank was met by a single, pungent odor that, sorted in his mind, became the smoky fragrance of hams and bacon, the toasty smell of crackers, the nose-tickling fragrances of pickles and onions, and above all, the fruity smell of dried apples, peaches, and apricots. His stomach rumbled with sudden hunger. Even the tobacco, bolts of cloth, and leather goods smelled pleasant.

Besides himself, the only other person in the store was a thin, aproned man seated behind the main counter, reading a newspaper. Hank licked his dry lips nervously, tasting salt. He cleared his throat.

The storeman peered at Hank over the tops of his spectacles. "What can I do for you?"

Hank went forward. "I'm lookin' for work," he said, one hand grasping the smooth countertop. "Could you use a boy to help you here in the store?" The man, reading again, seemed to be in no hurry to give him an answer. Hank shuffled his feet. "My folks an' me moved here a few months ago. We're farming ten miles out. But the drought—Pa wants a windmill—young'uns ain't eatin' right—"

The man waved for Hank to stop. "So you got troubles. Who hasn't? Mine is no customers." The storeman pointed to a sign behind him. "I'm stickin' with my policy, though, for a while yet. It may work."

Hank read the sign: "IN GOD WE TRUST, ALL OTHERS PAY CASH." He grinned and shrugged. "I reckon with no customers you don't need help."

"That's it in a persimmon pit." The storeman got up. "I'm sorry."

Hank watched the man hack a chunk from a wheel of yellow cheese. Coming around from behind the counter, the storekeeper dipped a hand into the cracker barrel and passed the cheese and crackers to Hank. "Sometimes I give out samples. When you're rich, bring your business to me."

Hank grinned and nodded. He backed across the plank floor, already sinking his teeth into creamy cheese and crisp cracker. "Will. All my trading. Be back," Hank assured with his mouth full.

BLAINE'S FLOUR AND FEED did not need him; the owner had three brawny sons to do his milling. Leaving there, Hank passed the saloon, without a doubt the busiest place of business this sweltering afternoon. Now, they could use a boy to wash glasses and sweep up, he thought to himself. In the same instant he pictured Mamma's reaction to his working in such a place, and the vision made his feet move faster. He crossed the street.

The PILLAR BANK was no place for him, either, Hank decided, peering through the door into the dusky interior. Just the thought of ciphering brought a feeling of panic to his middle.

Next to the bank was DELORIA'S FINE CLOHES FOR FINE LADIES, and next to that, THE SEW SHOPPE. Hank dismissed both of them with a snort. Ahead was the blacksmith shop, the only place of business left besides the jail across the street from it.

The blacksmith shop! Why hadn't he thought of it before? *Horses!* Hank grinned to himself and sniffed the air. *Horses!*

He approached the smithy, a sprawling, weather-beaten building with double doors opening wide to the outside. He noted with interest the pile of scrap iron—rods, broken tools, wheels, axles—at the side of one door, and by the other a pile of worn-out horseshoes so high he caught his breath, then whistled softly.

Inside, the banging of iron on iron was much louder. A cherry-red fire glowed in the forge. Hank, enjoying the rich smell of horses and hot iron, and fascinated by the deft skill of the blacksmith, who was repairing an iron wheel, put off his reason for being there and watched.

A while later the husky smith rolled the finished wheel aside and led forth a dappled mare from where it had been tethered in back. He stroked the horse, spoke softly to it, then cradled its left front hoof in his leather-aproned lap. With a buffer iron and hammer the smith's deft hands bent the clenches out and worked the shoe loose, pulling the old nails with pincers.

Seeing that the blacksmith wanted to toss the shoe into a pile behind him, Hank moved out of the way, but did not take his glance from the work. The smith gently scraped the hoof and pared it. Hank stepped in closer to watch the new shoe, heated at the forge, burn the hoof to an exact fit. Then, quickly, the smith plunged the shoe into a tub. Steam hissed from the bubbling water. The smith laid the cold shoe in place and set the nails. Then he twisted off the ends and clinched them tight.

Hank let out his breath. He had watched Pa shoe Lucy and Sal but there was something different in the way this black-haired giant did it. Like rasping the hoof smooth, making the edge even with the iron shoe. Might be the difference was that this was the smith's only trade, while Pa was a farmer and had to know a little bit about a lot of different things.

The mare began to move about, trying the feel of the new shoe, picking it up and setting it down on the floor. Again, Hank moved out of the way. The blacksmith was about to turn to still another chore when Hank remembered.

"I'm looking for work," he blurted. "Could you use somebody here? I'd do most anything."

The hairy arms crossed over the apron and the blacksmith whistled an almost soundless tune as he studied Hank. "Yes," he boomed finally. "My hired boy right now is my daughter, Zoe Vonna. She doesn't like the work."

"D-did you say yes?" Hank asked.

The blacksmith nodded. "Not that I can pay much." His voice had a deep echoing sound. "But I've got work. Errands to run, cleaning up, keeping a good fire. Sometimes I need help holding a nervous horse. Zoe Vonna does that, and turns the grindstone for me when I'm sharpening tools." He motioned with his head toward the big stone wheel in the far corner. "I know she'd like someone else around so she wouldn't have to leave off painting her pictures."

"I—I could do it. I could do it all!" Hank exclaimed.

"Twelve dollars a month be all right?" the blacksmith asked.

"Y-yes!" It was more than he'd hoped for. "I'm Hank Hedin. Is there a place around here where I can sleep? My home is quite a piece from here. I'd like to put my belongins' somewhere—" Hank broke off, thinking that he was spewing suddenly, like a teakettle.

The blacksmith grinned. "Go next door to my house. Tell Zoe Vonna to give you the back room." He held out a large hand. "Happy to have you with us, Hank. Zoe Vonna and me are known around here as the Mayfields."

The Mayfield cottage was a dwarf in the shade of the blacksmith shop. A picket fence encircled the tiny yard.

Hank hesitated at the gate, then hurried up the path to the vine-enclosed veranda. At his third knock, a girl opened the door.

"Wh-what is it?" she asked absentmindedly.

For an instant, Hank's glance fastened on the splotch of red paint on her nose. Then his blue eyes met her black ones. "I'm your Pa's new helper, Hank Hedin." He felt himself turning hot as lively interest replaced the faraway look on her face. Hank went on, "Mr. Mayfield says I'm to stay—here. A back room? I'm to leave my things."

"Oh." She held the door open for him. "I'm Zoe Vonna. The room is off the kitchen. It has just a cot and a chair in it. The view is nice, though. Your window looks out on the horse pasture in back, and the sunsets are really pretty."

Following her through the house, Hank could see that Zoe Vonna Mayfield's dark hair waved to her waist, and was tied back with a ribbon the same shade of red as the paint on her nose. "You paint pictures," he said. "Pictures of what?"

She smiled at him over her shoulder. "Horses. If you're going to work for Daddy—" she wrinkled her nose. "I spend too much time at the smithy, drawing horses."

In the kitchen, Zoe Vonna opened a door. "This is it."

There was a table next to the door and Hank froze beside it. On the table he saw a blue checkered cloth, daisies in a bottle, and a pie that smelled of hot apples.

Zoe Vonna smiled. "We're having fried chicken for supper tonight, too. Papa will want you to eat with us."

"Th-thank you," Hank murmured, feeling faint. He thought of rabbit stew and the family at home. His first trip back there he would take *good* things to eat, Hank decided.

~

WITHIN A MONTH, MR. MAYFIELD AND ZOE VONNA were like a second family to Hank, and Pillar was as familiar to him as the Hedin farm. His work at the smithy, even the hardest of it, was pleasure. Each morning, he rose early, had a quick breakfast with the Mayfields, then hurried to the blacksmith shop. For the next hour, he would split wood, feeling the rhythmic swing of the axe in his hands satisfying.

When the wood chopping was done he would fill the hearth with charcoal. Mr. Mayfield insisted on lighting the fire in the forge himself; it was a ritual with him. But it was up to Hank to work the huge bellows until the fire blazed.

From the first moment, Hank realized that handling the horses would be his favorite task for Mr. Mayfield. They never stopped coming—huge draft animals, handsome buggy horses, many work-weary nags, and now and then a half-wild mustang ridden by a cowboy who looked half-wild himself. The latter would cause Hank to begin dreaming again, longingly, of being a cowboy.

In the meantime, working in the blacksmith shop was almost as good. Except that Bigger ought to be with him, Hank argued silently to himself often. It wasn't fair for Bigger to miss out. If he could make Pa see it—If Mr. Mayfield was willing—

Finally, it was time for Hank's visit home. "I don't see harm in your friend visiting you here now and then," Mr. Mayfield said. "I can't hire him, too, even though I have work enough for two boys on occasion. Just haven't the cash to spare for wages."

Hank shrugged and frowned. "Pa might not want him to leave. He needs help, too." His voice lifted. "Bigger would love it, though. Horses and all. Someday we're goin' out West, to be cowboys."

"You and just about every boy from Kansas back east to the Atlantic Ocean." Mr. Mayfield grinned. He clapped a hand on Hank's shoulder. "Speaking of horses, there's no need in you walking all that way to see your folks. Take one of our horses. Speck is getting fat; she needs the workout. If your friend comes back with you, part of the time you can ride double."

Hank thanked the smith, and, taking his first month's pay, hurried to McCracken's. "I'm back to trade," he said. "Cash." Mr. McCracken put down the gazette he was reading. "I want butter beans," Hank said, "and flour, sugar, and dried apricots. Mamma can fix beans for supper and pie for after."

"All that?" Mr. McCracken's eyebrows lifted mockingly.

"Yeah. And peppermint candy for the kids." Hank couldn't help swaggering as he left the store. The family'd probably forgotten what really good eatin' was like.

As he headed the Mayfield's spotted mare along the road out of town a few minutes later, Hank's thoughts leaped ahead. He'd be glad to see Bigger and the family again, sure enough. He relaxed his hold on the reins and slapped the horse gently on the shoulder. "C'mon, Speck," he urged. She broke into a trot and the sun-baked prairie began to melt behind them into small puffs of dust.

Approaching the crumbling soddy that squatted in the

crook of Jimson Ridge, Hank was surprised to see smoke coming from the chimney.

His throat felt fried—he'd get a drink and meet the new folks, he decided. Hank reined in, dismounted, and ground-reined Speck. Nearing the open door, Hank stepped aside as a cloud of dust billowed out. From inside came coughing and swishing sounds.

Hank waited for the dust to settle, then said to the back of the man clearing the room with a stalk of broom-corn, "Howdy, just movin' in?" Hank stared at the hands gripping the stalk. Both thumbs were gone!

The scrawny fellow turned and Hank's glance moved up to the stranger's face. Hank drew a sharp, whistling breath. His heart felt as if it had stopped. The hawkish, sharp-eyed face peering from under a mop of black hair —it was the Scarecrow—from Missoura. Who *died* in the flood—only he couldn't have drowned. Here he was in Kansas! Hank reached for the doorframe and leaned against it to steady himself.

"Howdy yourself. Whatcha want?" the Scarecrow rasped.

"N-nothin. J-just nothin'," Hank stammered. "Howdyin' you, that's all." Stark fear sent chills racing up and down his spine. He motioned feebly for the Scare-crow to go on with his work and backed toward his horse.

The Scarecrow followed, his gaze piercing. "I seen you som'ers, before?" he questioned. "You allus live here, or are you from som'ers else? What's yer name?"

"N-name is Hank. Comin' from Pillar. I *live* yonder with my folks." If the Scarecrow didn't know they were the ones he had followed out of Missoura, he wasn't going to tell him. Hank whirled toward his horse.

"Hold on!" the Scarecrow yelled, running after him. "Don't guess I know you, but I want to ax you some questions. I'm lookin' fer a boy, name of Stokes. A towhead. Big boy, big nose, big hands. Seen anybody like that, around here?"

Bigger! The man wanted Bigger. Not the settling-up money from the farm, not their leavings in Missouri, or them. Why hadn't he seen it before! He was after *Bigger*.

Why? A bad thing, Hank felt certain. Hank was positive his bones had turned to mush, he found it so hard to walk to his horse and mount.

Forcing himself to look and feel calm, he said, "I don't reckon I know anybody like that. Why—what do you want him for?"

A look of cunning crossed the Scarecrow's face. Then it was gone. "Friends. We're friends," he said. "I know'd his Pa. Him and me used to be in the same b'ness. River clammers, we was. I fol—I mean, some folks on the road tol' me they seed a boy like Stokes headed this way. Thought I'd look him up. Ol' friends 'n all."

Hank swallowed. "Who's looking for this boy, if I do see him sometime?" he managed to get out.

"Varber. Chaw Varber." The Scarecrow coughed violently, then went on, "Charlton, after the town in West Virginia, is my real name. It got sawed off. Say," he exclaimed, his yellow eyes flashing, "don't you tell him I'm lookin' fer him." His voice turned to oil. "I want to surprise the young'un. It'd take the fun out of our meetin' if he was to know I'm looking fer 'im."

Hank stared down at the thumbless hand wrapped around his ankle. He shivered and pulled it away. The Scarecrow was still talking.

"Now, if this Stoke boy is aroun' an' you git wind of

it, jus' come let me know. I'll handle the rest. Big surprise, remember?"

Without answering, Hank nodded and turned his horse. He kneed her into a trot. Behind him, he heard Chaw Varber coughing.

The sound of coughing still echoed in his mind as he rode into the Hedin yard at a gallop and saw Johanna taking clothes from the line. He threw himself from the saddle and raced toward his sister. "Bigger," he blurted. "Where's Bigger? I got to talk to him!"

Johanna's look of surprise and delight turned to one of sympathy. "Bigger isn't here anymore, Hank," she said softly.

Chapter Seven

"Quit foolin', Johanna. You ain't funny," Hank said, feeling grim. "Is Bigger in the barn? The house? In the field somewhere? I got to see him now!"

Johanna chewed her lip. "I'm not funnin' you, Hank. Bigger is gone. He isn't here anymore. We don't know where he is."

Hank stared, panic knotting his insides. She was telling the truth! He grasped Johanna's shoulders and shook her. "Where? Where did Bigger go? What's happened to 'im?"

"Leave your sister be, Hank," Pa's voice boomed suddenly from behind him.

Hank turned. Pa and the younger girls, looking more ragged and thinner than when he had left, crossed the yard toward him. "Pa," Hank pleaded. "Where is he? Johanna says Bigger ain't here. You know where he is, don't you?"

Pa shrugged, and, looking at the ground, started to

speak. Just then Mamma came out of the house holding baby Lou Ella asleep against her. "Come inside, Son," she said gently. "Bigger did go away, but maybe he'll come back. He left one night without tellin' us—'course he can't talk, but—" Mamma's voice trailed off, and her face turned pink. "Pa and me think he felt bad about bein' an extra mouth to feed."

Hank shook his head, feeling numb. "He wouldn't go away, just like that. I don't think Bigger would do it. Did you go lookin' for him, Pa?" he asked, his voice thin. "Did you try to find him?"

Pa frowned, caught Hank by the arm, and moved him toward the house. "I did. We think a lot of Bigger, too, Son. Found traces where Bigger had been, down by the crick. Went north. Followed his trail most of a day, then lost it. I couldn't be sure it was his tracks, leavin', or old footprints of his'n from sometime when you and him were out, wandering around, playing. Wind stirs things up so."

"That's all?" Hank shouted, unable to keep his anger out of his voice. "That's all you did to get Bigger back?"

Pa's hand on Hank's arm tightened and he swung Hank around to face him. There was fire in Pa's eyes. His fuzzy eyebrows writhed. "I looked. I got the farm and the family to worry about. I didn't send the boy away. He was welcome here. I feel bad about his leavin', too, but I still say he left because he wanted to. Anytime he wants to come back, he has a home."

Hank's eyes stung; his throat filled. He swallowed. "I'm sorry, Pa." Hank moved toward Mamma and touched the baby's head with his forefinger. The silky touch of her hair went straight to his heart.

Inside the house, Hank tried to explain. "I got het up because Bigger is the only feller—he's the only friend I ever had. It—it don't seem right, hearin' you all sayin' so calm, 'Bigger is gone. We don't know where he is.'" Only then did Hank remember he hadn't told Pa about the Scarecrow.

Remembering brought a weak feeling to Hank's knees. He dropped into a chair. "Pa—" he began, "you know that old soddy just north of our line, in the crook of the ridge? It ain't empty now."

Although he had been hot and sweating, Hank felt cold inside when he began to talk about the new neighbor, Chaw Varber, the Scarecrow from Missouri. "He got out of the flood, somehow, and he's here lookin' for Bigger!" A sudden thought occurred to Hank. "Bigger left that cave and came with us to Kansas to get away from Varber, that's what!" he exclaimed.

"He stayed in the wagon with us girls," Elsa said in a hushed whisper, nodding agreement. "I didn't think he liked our games so much. He was tryin' to keep out of sight."

"His gettin' sick that time," Mamma wailed softly. "That happened right after you saw the stranger on the road, Hank."

Creases deepened in Pa's face. "He stomped the feller's hat in the mud when he thought he'd drowned. He got better after."

"One more thing, Pa," Hank said. "This Chaw Varber says he's good friends with Bigger Stokes, an' he tole just how he looks. But he left out somethin'. He didn't say nothin' about the fact that Bigger can't talk."

The long silence that followed was broken by

Johanna. "Do you think this Chaw Varber's comin' here has anything to do with Bigger bein' gone?" Her thin fingers nervously folded and unfolded the wash she had carried in.

Pa shook his head. "The boy has been gone two or three weeks. Hanks says this Varber feller just got here."

"No," Hank said, "Varber wouldn't of asked about Bigger the way he did, if he'd already seen 'im. Bigger must of gone off for some other reason. He must mean to come back." Hank felt better, saying it aloud. Still, there was the Scarecrow, Chaw Varber, to deal with. "We better tell the sheriff about Varber, right, Pa? Put him away so he don't go after Bigger, or get him when he tries to come back?"

Pa scratched his fingers through his wild red beard and then his hair. He spread his hands wide. "Tell the sheriff what? What do we know for *sure ?* The boy acted peculiar, so we been assumin' a lot of things. If Bigger could of talked, to tell us somethin' certain—" Pa scratched his head again. "What proof do we got that this man ain't what he says he is, a friend of Bigger Stokes?"

"Pa, I know!" Hank exploded. "Bigger was afraid of him. He didn't need to tell me." Hank swallowed hard. "I know. This—this Scarecrow, he's got these yellowish eyes, he ain't got no thumb on either hand—"

Pa interrupted, "Hank, the way the feller looks ain't proof of nothing. All we got to go on is our own guessin'. Pshaw! The man could be innocent as a newborn babe for all the actual proof we got."

"That's right, Hank," Mamma chided. "You oughten to judge folks by the way they look. Son," she said, her voice lifting, "you haven't told us yet, but you must of found work in Pillar. What are you doin' there? Whose horse are you ridin'?"

It was next to impossible to turn his mind away from Bigger, but gradually Hank got out the story of his work at the smithy, and his home with the Mayfields. "I like it a lot," he added. "Here's my pay, Pa, 'cept for a little I spent on candy an' supper. Thunderin' toads, I forgot. I was so addled at findin' the Scarecrow in the Jimson Ridge shack I didn't think to put Speck, Mr. Mayfield's horse, up. Twinny," he said, giving Dixie's pigtail a yank, "you come carry in the vittles."

Leading the horse to the barn, Hank became aware of Pa following close behind. "Your workin' and earnin' cash money is mighty important to us, Hank," Pa said. "I think we'll be able to plant some of that Red Turkey winter wheat like Mennonites been doin' so good with. I'm goin' to Newton soon as I can to dicker for seed."

Hank nodded, half of his mind far away. Inside the earthy smelling barn, Hank unsaddled Speck, gave her hay, then faced Pa. "I want to go look for Bigger. What if he's somewhere hungry, by himself, and scared out of his wits like before in Missoura?" Hank's glance followed anxiously as Pa, without answering, led the way out again into bright sunlight.

Pa kept walking, his hands a gnarled ball behind him. Finally, he turned. "No. That's why I'm tellin' you your workin' is important. I knowed you'd want to go look for him." Pa's chin lifted. "As long as this Mayfield feller will give you work in his blacksmith shop, you got to take it."

For a moment, Hank stood there, feeling nothing, until Pa's words sunk in. "Got to get a drink of water,

Pa," he gasped then, moving by him fast so Pa wouldn't see in his face the fury he was feeling.

"If I need you to come home, I'll send for you," Pa shouted after him. "Other than that, 'long as I can git by without you, you got to work for wages."

Hank's throat was still tight with anger at suppertime, and he found that the meal he had so eagerly bought the makings for would not go down. When someone spoke to him, he mumbled back, hardly knowing what he was saying, or whom he was talking to. Then the miserable visit was over. It was time to go back to Pillar.

AS HE RODE BY THE NEXT DAY, THE JIMSON RIDGE SHACK looked temporarily deserted. Was the Scarecrow out hunting for Bigger? It was all Hank could do to keep the horse, Speck, on the road to Pillar. He longed desperately to strike off on a search for Bigger. If only he could have a chance to look for him, to warn Bigger that Chaw Varber was alive and—

Pa, though, said he had to WORK. Hank drooped lower in the saddle and rode on.

"Hank," Mr. Mayfield pleaded later in the shop, "get this crowbait off me!"

Hank grabbed the horses's halter and pulled her from her leaning stance against the blacksmith. He had to stop worrying about Bigger or he might lose his job, Hank thought with dismay. "You got three legs free to stand on. Use 'em!" he hissed into the horse's ear. "Mr. Mayfield can't give your hind hoof a new shoe and hold you up, too."

But where had Bigger gone? Hank relaxed his grasp

on the mare's halter. Too late, he felt her swing her head free. She gave Mr. Mayfield's back a spiteful nudge with her nose, almost knocking the blacksmith over. Hank groaned and swiftly caught her head. "Sorry, Mr. Mayfield."

"Your mind is not on your work, Hank," Mr. Mayfield said firmly. "Fretting about that mute boy you told Zoe Vonna and me about?"

"Y-yes," Hank confessed. "I try not to think about it all the time. But Bigger just up and disappeared—I can't figure out why—"

"I think your friend will come back," a new voice interrupted from behind them. "And you'll know then, Hank, why he went away."

It was Zoe Vonna. Hank grinned his gratitude. "You ought to draw a picture of this lazy no 'count Nellie."

Zoe Vonna laughed. "I will sometime. As soon as you two finish with her, come for supper."

At twilight Hank sat with Zoe Vonna on the front porch to get away from the stifling heat of the house. "Sing with me," she urged. "We won't notice how awful hot it is."

They harmonized, his almost-man's bass and her soprano: "Sing, who-o, who-o, whoop, cows away..."

It was Mamma's cowboy song. Zoe Vonna said the name of it was "The Pecos Stream." She taught Hank more words to it. While Hank sang, it was easy to picture himself riding herd in the cool shade of tall trees along a stream. He wasn't riding alone. Hank stopped singing.

"Thinking of your friend, Bigger, again?" Zoe Vonna asked softly. "Don't fret so, Hank. I have a feeling it will all come out all right."

Hank nodded. For a long time he and Zoe Vonna sat

without talking. It was uncommon, he thought, since Zoe Vonna was a *girl*, but she seemed to understand, more than anyone else, how he felt about Bigger's disappearance. Or maybe it was that she made him feel hopeful.

A short time later, forks of dry lightning stabbed the purple darkness. "Looks and smells like rain," Hank murmured, breaking the silence. "I reckon Pa will send for me to come home and help him farm again."

By morning, it was raining hard, and did not let up all day. The streets of Pillar turned into a quagmire. Hank grinned as he watched youngsters, old folks, and townspeople of all ages in between slog to and from their assorted errands with revived joy and hope on their faces. He was not surprised when Johanna came for him the next day.

"In here, Sis," he called out, seeing Johanna's shy, uncertain movements as she slid from Lucy's back in front of the smithy.

Johanna's face brightened when she saw him. She ran to Hank and grabbed his hands. "Axle grease," he said, trying to draw them back.

She held them anyway, saying, "Isn't the rain wonderful, Hank?" She brushed back an auburn curl, leaving a dark streak on her cheek. "Pa can work the hard old ground now, and the wheat has a chance. But he needs you home to help plant and all," Johanna said.

Hank nodded. "Mr. Mayfield is busy, too. But I told him Pa might want me home. We'd better tell him you've come. He's at home right now, having coffee. Johanna—?"

Before he could finish, Johanna answered the question Hank was burning to know. "No," she said, her pretty face solemn. "Bigger hasn't come back. We haven't heard a word."

Worry about Bigger, always with him, deepened at Johanna's words. "What about—Varber? The feller at Jimson Ridge?" he asked.

"Comes and goes," Johanna told him. "We've only seen him a time or two. Most of the time he's gone off somewhere. Maybe he works. I don't know how he lives, otherwise."

Off somewhere huntin' for Bigger, probably, Hank thought. Or out stealin' for his livin'; that was more like Varber. "C'mon," Hank mumbled, leading Johanna toward the Mayfield cottage.

Mr. Mayfield's eyes softened as he looked at Johanna and heard Hank out. "I'll check the hotel for drifters holed up out of the rain, and hire one if I can." He motioned for Hank and Johanna to join him at the table. "Your sister needs a rest, Hank, and a chance to dry out."

Hank watched appreciatively as Zoe Vonna placed cups of steaming coffee in front of them, along with deep dishes of wild plum cobbler.

Later, as Hank and Johanna prepared to leave, Zoe Vonna said, blushing, "I hope you'll be back before too long, Hank."

Hank felt his own face grow warm. His glance clung to Zoe Vonna's for just an instant. He grabbed his sister's elbow roughly. "C'mon, old maid." Outside, Hank chuckled, for no reason he could think of except that he felt good. He put an arm across Johanna's shoulders. "Sis," he said, "a good-lookin' gal like you ought to have a beau. You want me to find you one?"

In the circle of his arm, Johanna stiffened. She glared

at him, whatever she was trying to say obviously stuck in her throat. Her violet eyes glistened.

Thunderin' toads, Hank thought, Johanna does want a beau and she doesn't think it's funny. "Wait!" he yelled, as she bolted away. He followed as Johanna raced to Lucy, tethered in front of the blacksmith shop. In seconds, Johanna had mounted and turned Lucy onto the road out of town.

Hank followed on foot down the muddy road. Johanna was soon a small moving object far ahead, but the words she shouted back at Hank were very clear. "I'll teach you to call me an old maid!"

For a time, the sky was clear and Hank could see for miles in every direction. "I'm wearin' this road out," he grumbled aloud in self-pity. "Back and forth. Home, to Pillar. Pillar, to home. A waste of time. I oughtta be out lookin' for Bigger!" It began to shower, enclosing him in a small gray world. Now and then the prairie shook with thunder. Streaks of lightning fired the sky.

Hank walked with eyes half-closed, shoulders scrunched forward, thinking of the days of hard work waiting for him at the farm. It would be uncommonly awful, with Bigger not there.

An edgy feeling came over Hank. He turned his head and drew a sharp breath. He was being followed! Hank quickened his steps and sneaked a second look at the shadowy figure on muleback. Was it Chaw Varber? It looked like a scarecrow sitting on a mule. Whoever it was, he was giving him a good look-see. Like a coyote ready to pick off a cottontail rabbit, Hank thought.

He couldn't talk to Chaw Varber; the Scarecrow might cause him to give away something about Bigger! Hank broke into a run. The clay mud of the road clung to his feet like glue and made moving fast next to impossible. Hank struggled on, but a look over his shoulder told him his follower was moving faster, every mule stride a gain.

It was Varber, Hank felt sure. For a sickening instant, Hank was afraid he was being run down. He lurched to one side, lost his footing, and fell headlong into the mud. He sat up, his heart pounding furiously, his ears recognizing Chaw Varber's strangling cough. Hank clawed at the mud that was blinding him.

"Wipe all that mud off so I can see who you be," Varber snarled.

"It's m-me." Hank spat. "Hank Hedin. Leave me alone. I ain't done nothing." He struggled to his feet and began to walk backward in the direction of home. "My Pa's comin' to meet me," he lied. "Oughtta be here any minute now."

"I thought you was somebody I knowed," Chaw Varber snapped, then coughed.

"Who?" Hank demanded, squinting up at Varber. "That—that Stokes boy you talked about? You ain't found him?" While looking for an answer in the hawkish face coming toward him, Hank discovered something else. Varber was sick. Bad sick. His face was as gray as a horse blanket, and his yellow eyes looked glassy.

Still, Hank had to know. "You ever find that Stokes boy you were looking for?"

Chaw Varber's answer was lost in a fit of coughing.

Hank waited, scarcely daring to breathe. Varber tried again to speak, and failed. Hank started forward as Varber almost fell from the mule.

"You oughtta get on home; you're sick," Hank blurted.

Varber nodded, still coughing. "Tell—your Mamma. She got medicine? Tell—" He stretched out over the mule's neck and slapped its shoulder. "Git, git on," he mumbled, turning the mule.

Hank watched Chaw Varber disappear into the gray drizzle in the direction of his shack. If he didn't feel deeply sure that Chaw Varber was a terrible danger for Bigger Stokes, he might be sorry for the sick man. As it was, he didn't feel hardly anything, Hank decided.

Turning on legs that felt like two dead stumps, Hank continued toward home. After a few steps he saw a horse loping toward him. Johanna. Saying nothing, she halted Lucy beside him and motioned for Hank to climb up behind her. Hank grinned tiredly at his older sister. She knew he hadn't hurt her feelings on purpose. Otherwise she wouldn't have come back for him.

THE DAYS THAT FOLLOWED WERE SO BUSY FOR HANK IT seemed there were no nights, only long, steamy days following Pa's breaking plow, broadcasting by hand the wheat seed he carried in a heavy pouch slung from his shoulder. After he did the broadcasting, the team pulled a brush drag over it, harrowing the seed under.

The work was hard and slow, causing Pa to talk at night of mortgages to buy machinery that would make the work easier and faster. Pa talked, too, of buying more land and planting bigger crops to earn bigger profits. At such times, Hank, bone-weary and bored with "farm talk," would turn in and try to sleep. But when Pa talked farming, he talked loud. Hank was sure he could be heard for miles.

One night, unable to fall asleep, Hank suddenly remembered that Chaw Varber had asked for medicine. Slowly, Hank sat up. He had forgotten, clean forgotten! What if Varber had—had died? Hank's skin crawled. Wrapping a blanket around him, he went to the kitchen, where Mamma was setting yeast to rise for tomorrow's baking.

Chapter Eight

Mamma listened, then clutched Hank's shoulders. "The man for sure has pneumonia! He was in that flood—" Her face came close to study Hank's. "Son, if you didn't tell me because of Bigger—why, that's murder, practically."

She turned from him without waiting for a reply. "We reach out the hand of friendship to everyone," she said, climbing onto a chair in front of the cupboard, "and we don't know for sure that Mr. Varber means Bigger harm."

Hank didn't argue but watched as Mamma chose carefully from her small treasure of medicines, then climbed down. A half-bottle of Dr. Easterley's Fever and Ague Killer, calomel, and a packet of ginger for tea went into her satchel.

"Hitch Lucy and Sal to the wagon," she ordered, shoving Hank toward the door. "I'll tell your pa where we're goin'."

Hank struggled against her firm hand and darted back under Mamma's arm. "I got to get more clothes on!" he protested.

Obeying Mamma's orders, Hank drove across the moonlit prairie. In what seemed no time at all, they reached Varber's shanty. Hank gasped when he saw the white cloth fluttering from the door latch. A signal for help!

"You ought to be ashamed, Hank," Mamma cried. "What if we're too late?"

It was pitch-dark and bad-smelling inside the soddy. "I'll find the t-table and light the l-lamp." Hank dug in his pocket for a match.

The soft glow of light showed Chaw Varber in bed at the far side of the room. Mamma nodded. "He's alive. Cot's shakin' from his chills and shiverin'. Find somethin' more to cover him, Hank. Bring his coat there, by the door. Build a fire and heat some water."

Varber coughed, and it sounded to Hank as though the man's chest would rip open. When the coughing ended, Hank expected Varber's breathing to stop, too, but it didn't.

Soon, Mamma leaned over the bed, patiently spooning medicine between his yellow lips. Hank stood by, holding the steaming cupful of ginger tea that was to follow.

"We can't leave him," Mamma whispered, as the hours stretched toward dawn. "The Lord knows he's got to have some mortal standin' by."

Hank made coffee. They sat at Varber's table. Hank's eyes burned and his head ached from lack of sleep, but he didn't want Mamma nursing Varber alone. After a while, he said quietly, "Mamma, I did forget about Varber ailing. We got so busy plantin' right off as soon as I got home. I didn't do this apurpose."

Mamma squeezed his arm. "Oh, Hank, I was just

prattlin'. I know my boy better than that when I think about it. We'll do the best we can by our neighbor. That's all we can do. If the Lord decides—"

"He still might—might die?" Hank worried. "Mamma, I don't want him to. Even if he is a low-down, snake-rattlin' Jonah, I don't want him to die like this on my account."

Mamma shook her head, frowning. "Hank, you know I don't abide name-callin', so no more of it."

The long silence that followed was broken by sick murmurings from the bed. "He's addled from fever," Mamma said, getting to her feet. "Make more tea. We got to make him sweat. The fever's got to come down."

Hank listened, trying to make something from the garbled ramblings. Chill bumps raced up and down his spine. He could understand nothing.

Suddenly, Chaw Varber began to scream, a chain of words that almost brought Hank to his knees from shock. "Mine! Rich, rich. Give it—BIG. BIG!"

Big, *Bigger*. Hank moved slowly toward the bed. Was Varber talking about Bigger, about Bigger Stokes? "What are you talking about?" He grabbed Chaw Varber's arm and shook him. "What about Bigger? Have you hurt him? Tell me!" Mamma tried to pull him away from the bed, but Hank jerked out of her grasp and crouched by the bed. "Where is he?" he pleaded. "Tell me what you've done to him!"

Hank fell back in horror as Chaw Varber struggled to rise, a look of maniacal joy twisting his face. "Biggest one!" he shrilled. "Biggest ever!"

Not Bigger Stokes. Just something big Varber was seeing in his wild dreaming. That's what his talk was about. Unsteadily, Hank got to his feet, stumbled to a chair, and dropped into it. That might mean Bigger was still all right. Hank buried his face in his arms, thankful.

~

LATER, HANK WOKE TO FIND HIMSELF ON THE FLOOR, Mamma's shawl over him. "Wh-what happened?" he asked, seeing Mamma at the table smiling at him.

"You've slept nigh all day," she said. "But you had the right. You helped save a human life last night." Mamma motioned with her head toward Varber. "The fever broke."

Hank looked, saw the quilt over Chaw Varber's chest moving up and down with easy regularity. Behind the man's skin, there appeared to be life where it had looked to be ending earlier. "Thunderin' toads," Hank mumbled. He grinned at Mamma. "Far as I'm concerned, the feller's still goin' to get what he's got comin' to him, but I'm glad he didn't die of pneumonia 'cause of me."

"He'll be all right, now," Mamma said. "I baked for him and made a soup from about everythin' I found. It'll last several days. He'll be able to take care of himself."

Going home, Mamma drew her shawl about her tighter. "The good, warm days are about over." Her teeth chattered as she added, "And I do dread winter so."

~

DIGGING DOWN IN THE WELL HOLE ONE NOVEMBER morning as the wind whipped across the prairie above him, Hank remembered Mamma's words. Winter always seemed to bring the same kind of troubles. Like sickness.

Even now, baby Lou Ella was ailing, though no doubt Mamma would bring her through it fine.

What did winter have in store for Bigger, wherever he was? Sometimes Hank wondered if he would ever see Bigger again. If only he could go look for him. Borrow a saddle horse from Mr. Mayfield, and go from town to town, farm to farm, asking questions. Sooner or later, somebody'd be sure to say, "Yep, I know the boy you're speakin' of. A strange one. Never talked. Appeared to be runnin' from somebody. He went—"

Here, Hank's dream of finding Bigger faded away, as it always did. Where, where, where? he tortured himself with the question. *Why* did Bigger go? Grinding his lip between his teeth, Hank viciously attacked the dirt wall with the shovel. He stopped suddenly. Had somebody called to him? He listened.

"Hello, the house!"

Someone was out there! Hank climbed swiftly from the well hole to look. A buggy was stopping in front of the house. A happy shout exploded from Hank. "Hey!" He grinned broadly. "H'lo folks. Mr. Mayfield, Zoe Vonna." He ran forward, wiping his dirty hands on his overalls. He eagerly helped Zoe Vonna down, shook Mr. Mayfield's hand, then rushed to unhitch their sorrel buggy horse, Sadie.

He led the Mayfields self-consciously toward the stone house, and inside made them known to the members of his family. "I'm sorry I ain't been back," he told the blacksmith and his daughter, "but Pa's needed me right along. What—?"

"Everything is fine," Mr. Mayfield boomed, a sweep of his huge palm doing away with Hank's worry. "I hired a journeying smith who was passing through. He's decided to spend the winter. Left him in charge today. Sweetheart," he nodded at Zoe Vonna, "you tell the folks why we've come."

While she talked, Zoe Vonna's dark eyes traveled from person to person but kept coming back to Hank. "A Christmas celebration," she said. "Before everybody gets snowed in for the winter. It will be held in the Pillar schoolhouse two weeks before Christmas. Those who can are to bring a special dish or two. We will have games, singing, and dancing. You all can come, can't you?" she finished breathlessly.

Hank's tongue was dry and wouldn't work, so he just nodded, hard.

"Come to a celebration?" Mamma exclaimed, clapping her hands. "We most certainly will. My, it's been ages since I've danced—" Her voice trailed off and her face went crimson. "Goodness, I nearly forgot. The baby is ailin'. I won't be goin', I reckon."

"Pshaw!" Hank's father snorted. "If there's dancing, Nin, honey, you're going. I'll stay home if need be."

Mr. Mayfield's laugh thundered around the room. "Let's get the babe well so you can all be there," he said. "I know folks living so far from town are bound to run out of things, so I took it upon myself to collect some supplies for you. Foodstuff. And Mr. McCracken sent a bit of quinine. Says he doesn't want his customers dying off like last winter. The quinine should fix our babe. Hank, you want to bring the packages in out of the wagon?"

As he started for the door, Hank saw Zoe Vonna voluntarily rise as if to follow, then she blushed and sat down again. "Zoe Vonna," Hank croaked, "come help me." Everyone stared as she flew after him but Hank discovered he felt more proud than anything.

Outside, loading his arms beside the wagon, Hank saw that Zoe Vonna was frowning nervously. She opened her mouth, closed it, then opened it again. He stepped nearer. "What's the matter?"

Her hand was light on his arm. "I-I d-didn't know if I should tell you. It may be nothing and I don't want you to get your hopes up, then be disappointed. But this traveling blacksmith Papa hired mentioned a mute boy he ate dinner with on the trail one night. It was weeks ago, in the Smoky Hill country up north."

There was a loud pounding in Hank's head, and he gripped the packages to keep from dropping them. "Bigger? Was it Bigger?"

"Oh, Hank, I don't know," Zoe Vonna cried. "The blacksmith just told of stopping at this campfire. He said there was a boy who couldn't talk, and an old man, a horse wrangler. I asked all the questions I could think of, Hank. He said the boy was all right, and seemed to be there of his own free will. He couldn't remember what he looked like, because he only spent about an hour with them."

A long, ragged sigh escaped Hank. "It was him. I bet anything it was Bigger. Hiding out, maybe. Thunderin' toads, if I just knew how to get rid of Chaw Varber, I could go get Bigger. I could bring him home! Maybe Bigger *knows* that Varber is hanging around, squatting just above our property line, waiting for him to come back." Pain glazed his eyes until Hank could hardly see the girl in front of him. "There is somethin' awful between Chaw Varber and Bigger," he choked, "I feel it in my soul, Zoe Vonna."

Her eyes were sympathetic. "I know, Hank, I know. Believe that everything will turn out all right, though. I'm positive it will." She shivered. "We-we better go in."

"I got to do something," he told her in a low, harried voice, going to the house. "I got to do something about Chaw Varber. He's been sick, but last Pa checked, Varber, he said, was gettin' strong as a buck deer. I reckon that means he's gettin' as dangerous as a painter, too."

As the days passed, Hank thought of several ways to encourage Chaw Varber to quit the country. He had heard things—like, you could pour gunpowder or sulphur down the chimney into a man's fire. Hank worked up just about enough courage for an attack on the Jimson Ridge shack, but then realized he had neither gunpowder or sulphur. Besides, it seemed to him that Mamma kept an eagle eye on him nowadays, and what he had on his mind came nowhere near Mamma's law that you treat your neighbor, no matter who he is, kindly.

THE DAY FOR THE CHRISTMAS CELEBRATION ARRIVED, cold and gray. Baby Lou Ella had recovered and the whole family crowded into the wagon. As it creaked toward Pillar, Hank half-listened to Pa's hopeful talk of weather. "A blanket of snow will keep the wheat sprouts warm in the ground," he said. "It'll hold 'em just so till time for 'em to shoot out of the ground come spring."

"Yeah, Pa," Hank mumbled. His gaze was fastened on the barren prairie stretching northwestward. Was Bigger off there somewhere? Was *he* the boy by the campfire who couldn't talk? Or was Bigger someplace else? Maybe, Hank thought, Bigger had already been done in and was underground like Pa's winter wheat. Hank briskly rubbed a sleeve across his forehead in a vain effort to wipe away his unhappy thoughts.

As they neared town, Hank saw that wagons, buggies, and people on horseback were coming into Pillar from all directions. Hank's feeling of gloom lessened when he spotted the Mayfields alighting from their buggy at the school. He took Sadie, Lucy, and Sal, and led them into the shed, where other horses were already lined at the long hay rack in back. Laughing, shouting people, many he had met during his stay in Pillar, some complete strangers, were hurrying for the schoolhouse door to be out of the sharp cold.

Checking the wagon, Hank found that Pa had gotten Mamma's Dutch oven full of fricasseed prairie chicken and fat white noodles to take inside. Hank drew his stomach in tight toward his backbone to still the hungry rumbling as Johanna and Elsa passed with two dried apple pies. He spotted the twins arguing to see who would carry their one small dish of molasses taffy. Stout little Dixie won, as he knew she would.

A sudden feeling of sympathy, that surprised him, caused Hank to take Clover's hand in his. "Let's go in and see if they got a Christmas tree," he said gruffly. He felt, more than saw, that Zoe Vonna had joined them. Hank smiled down at her. "I don't reckon that feller who works for your Pa has remembered anything else?"

Zoe Vonna shook her head. There was apology in the black eyes that looked up at him. Her slender fingers kneaded the ribbons of her gray bonnet. "When I talked to him again, he said the boy might not have been a mute at all. He said the boy didn't utter a word while he was there, and he did think so at the time. He—he isn't sure, now."

They had reached the door, so Hank didn't voice his disappointment. The little hand in his gripped tighter and he heard himself exclaim, "Will you look at that!"

Muslin, dyed red and green, was draped everywhere —above the many windows that circled the schoolroom, on the tables, and from the rafters.

"Anything wrong?" Zoe Vonna giggled.

"No. Nothin'. I just never saw Christmas so—so Christmasy. Somebody went to a mite of trouble," Hank told her.

"It was fun," Zoe Vonna said, her voice bubbly. "Papa says he'll have to shoe one hundred horses to pay for the muslin. But some of the women in town will buy it for dressmaking. And I want to give some to your sisters."

"Look at the Christmas tree, Clove," Hank said, laughing loud. The tree was a thickety wild plum, naked of greenery, but heavily adorned with harness buckles, bells, spur chains, bits, and, at the top of the tree— competing mightily with the real North Star—was a cluster of shiny silver harness rosettes.

"I have to take everything back to the shop after," Zoe Vonna explained. "Does—does it look silly, Hank?"

He shook his head, quickly sobering. For a long time he hadn't felt so warm inside as he did just now. "It's nice—, Zoe Vonna. With the lamps shining on it, it looks —like a Christmas tree ought to look. Shining bright and pretty." Clover's head, at his elbow, bobbed vigorously.

"Find Mamma and show her," Hank said, and Clover zipped away. When something brushed his other hand, Hank looked down and saw that Zoe Vonna was giving him a flat package.

"Merry Christmas." She smiled and looked at the floor.

Hank untied the ribbon and removed the paper. "Thunderin' toads, it's me!" He held the picture away from him, seeing all the small details: the blacksmith shop with himself in front holding the head of a white stallion. The piles of scrap iron were there by the doors. Inside, in the blue shadows of the shop, was Mr. Mayfield at the forge.

In a moment, Hank could speak. "It's fine, Zoe Vonna, so fine. I—I never knew a person could draw as —as—You remembered everything. The picture is—like real."

"You're welcome," Zoe Vonna answered, her eyes twinkling.

"I ain't got a thing for you," he said. "Not a thing. But someday—" Hank's face burned. "Merry Christmas, Zoe Vonna."

After dinner, Zoe Vonna went to help with clearing away and Hank sat on a bench along the wall, watching the lively dancers in the middle of the room. He rubbed his stomach and wondered how any of them could move. Words to the fiddle tune spun in his brain:

"Where, O where is sweet lit-tie Nel-lie? Way down yon-der in the pawpaw patch."

Pa had eaten every bit as much of the holiday feast as he had, Hank concluded, but Mamma had him out on the floor spinning like a spring tornado. Johanna and Elsa, for the moment, partnered one another. Several young men had their eyes on them, though, on Johanna, for certain. Hank drew a sharp breath. One of the watching men was Chaw Varber!

When had Varber come in? He looked fit as a fiddle,

too. Anyone who really knew what he was wouldn't have invited him here, Hank told himself. But then, maybe nobody did invite him.

Hank came off the bench as Varber elbowed others out of the way, separated Elsa from Johanna, and grasped the older girl's arm roughly.

Zoe Vonna, a white apron over her soft gray dress, came hurrying to Hank's side. "Is that the man who is after your friend, Bigger?" she asked. "The awful-faced one dancing with Johanna?"

"Yeah," Hank growled. "What's he sayin' to her anyway? Been talkin' a mile a minute ever since he got hold of her."

"I—I don't think your sister likes it, whatever he is talking about," Zoe Vonna said worriedly.

Several minutes passed. Then Johanna frowned, twisted free of Varber's grip on her arm, and came hurrying toward Hank and Zoe Vonna.

Hank shivered inwardly when he saw the queer mixture of satisfaction and displeasure on Varber's face as he looked after Johanna.

"What's the matter, Sis? What's Varber bothering you for?"

Johanna bit her lip and sat down, shaking her head. Her hand shook as she pushed an auburn curl behind her ear. "It's—it's—he keeps wantin' to know where Bigger is," she said finally.

Hank let out an explosive breath and his heart thudded. "You!" he choked. "Varber is asking *you* about Bigger, Johanna? Why you?"

"I—I let it slip," Johanna cried. "He was talking about— about Mamma being such a good doctor, getting him over pneumonia. I was nervous; afraid of him. I wasn't thinking. Just talking—I-I told about Mamma taking care of B-Bigger on—on the trail from Missoura. Oh, Hank, I'm sorry."

His secret was out. Hank felt very tired. His tongue was strangely numb in his mouth; his heartbeat even seemed to slow. The girls were watching him, their eyes questioning and worried. Across the room Chaw Varber smirked, then slowly came toward them.

Hank watched him come, thinking how different this Scarecrow looked from the innocent kind that hung from a stake in the garden. The vision swam and Hank was aware only of an evil grin and, below it, black cloth coiling and worming closer and closer.

Hank forced himself up to his tallest height, and through tight lips said, "Chaw Varber didn't know for sure 'til now that we know Bigger Stokes, that we brought Bigger from Missoura. I reckon he suspicioned it though, or he wouldn't of been staying so close all this time. It's all right, Sis," he said quietly. "I reckon it *is* better, gettin' things out in the open. Let *'em* start something here an' now if he wants!"

Chapter Nine

"**M**r. Varber?" Hank was amazed that he could smile as he spoke. "You're lookin' fit. My sister, Johanna, says you got some questions about Bigger Stokes?"

Satisfaction welled in Hank at Varber's startled expression, which quickly turned to one of suspicion. A foot in front of Hank, the Scarecrow halted. "Tell me where he is." Chaw Varber's order was icy with threat.

"Don't know," Hank said. "An' I'll tell you somethin' else. I'm *glad* I don't know. 'Cause that way, there ain't nothin' you can do or say to me an' my sister that'll make us tell you somethin' we just plain ain't got the answer to."

Hank waited, breathing deeply. The gray cloth of Zoe Vonna's dress brushed his left arm. Close on his right was the deep blue of Johanna's dress. He was aware of their soft, fearful breathing. Others in the room faded into the background. "Well?" Hank asked.

Chaw Varber stroked his long jaw with a thumbless hand. His eyes glinted like dirty yellow brass. "You lied to me afore, said you didn't know Bigger Stokes," he accused. "You're probably lyin' now 'bout where he is."

Hank shook his head. "I am not. An' while we're at it, what about you sayin' Bigger is a friend of yours? He ain't, is he? You want him for somethin'." Hank took a deep breath. "Maybe you even want to—" For the life of him, Hank couldn't say the word "kill" aloud. He held his ground as Varber brought his whiskery face close.

The Scarecrow's right shoulder began to jerk. He started to say something, then his face took on a look as closed as a dead man's. Abruptly, he turned and left the schoolhouse.

Hank waited until he was gone, then stumbled to the bench and sat down.

With her arm held tight across her stomach, Zoe Vonna cried after a moment, "Oh, that man! Something about him gives me the chills."

Johanna, eyes closed, stood stiffly in one spot. She uttered one word. "Evil!"

The party drew to an end a short time later. Tired, cold, and filled with apprehension, Hank kept a careful watch going home. But he saw no sign of Chaw Varber.

OFTEN, HOWEVER, IN THE GRAY, CHILLING DAYS THAT followed, Hank saw the Scarecrow on his mule, watching the stone house from Jimson Ridge. "Fool!" Hank yelled once, seeing him there. Chaw Varber stuck out like a cut thumb. Did he think Bigger would come to the house and get caught? "If I can see you so plain," Hank hissed aloud, "Bigger will be able to, too. Bigger Stokes will outsmart you to the end; wait and see!"

What was easy to say was not easy to believe. Then, other worries joined Hank's concern for Bigger. On a day in February, it began to snow in earnest, and at midday, Hank went to the sod barn to gauge their wood supply. Not enough if they had a blizzard and couldn't get out for more, he decided. Like food, there was never enough wood, really.

Pa was on top of the house, patching the roof. Hank could scarcely see him through the swirling white. Hank shouted, cupping his hands around his mouth, "Pa, don't you think I ought to take Lucy and the wagon an' scour the crick bank for more wood?"

Pa's heavy beard was white with snow as he looked down. He was silent, considering, then answered, "All right. Be careful, though. Don't never git out of sight of the house. Can't trust weather like this. Gettin' lost is easy. I'd go myself but I got to finish this roof. There's a thin place a heavy snow would cave in, sure."

"I can do it, Pa," Hank shouted back.

Hank searched until almost dark, checking now and then to see if he could still make out the forlorn-looking house, a dark lump in the blowing white. As time passed, his flesh ached with cold, then numbed until he could feel nothing.

Later, the few pieces of wood he found thumped and bumped behind him in the wagon bed as he struck back toward home. Pa had tied a rope from the barn to the house, ready if a real blizzard came. Hank put the team up and followed the rope to the house.

Over supper he told Pa, "I'll have to go further if I'm goin' to find anywhere near enough wood. Snowing like it is, I'll have to dig for it. Pa—" Hank couldn't find words for the desperation he was feeling.

"I wish," Pa said, "I'd had you girls out on the prairie afore this, picking up cow chips. There's been cattle drives through west of here; you could have taken the wagon and got a load or two."

The twins looked at one another, wrinkling their noses and touching the tips of their tongues to their chins. "Peuw," Dixie said, wriggling, "pick up—"

"I'd have done it," Elsa interrupted solemnly. "I wish you'd thought of it sooner, Pa. In times of need, people often have to do uncommon things."

Johanna broke in, "I wish we had moved to Kansas City. Anywhere where there's people, and fine things, and factory jobs—"

The outburst was so unlike Johanna that every head at the table turned toward her. Hank swallowed hard when he saw the mist clouding her violet eyes. Her face was chalk-white. Johanna was scared, he realized. Scared of being stranded 'way out here on the prairie with bad weather coming and not enough of anything they needed. In Missoura they had always had plenty of wood, garden truck in the root cellar, and fresh venison.

Mamma's eyes flashed. But there was gentle understanding behind the firmness of her voice. *"Pa* chose Kansas. Kansas it is. Fanciful wishing can be saved for when there's nothin' better to do."

Johanna got up from the table, covered her face with her hands, and flew from the room, sobbing.

"She don't mean it," Hank said quickly. "Not what she said. Johanna is—is worried we—we won't manage to—keep alive. Not enough wood. Food low."

A heavy silence followed his words. Tears trickled down Clover's cheeks. Dixie stared at her empty plate as though she would be seeing it that way always. Pa and

Mamma looked at one another, saying nothing. In the far corner of the room, the baby stirred and made a soft mewing sound.

"Well, thunderin' toads," Hank choked out, "I didn't mean to strike everybody dumb. We got us a snowstorm. So what? Johanna don't stop to think that people come through worse than this all the time. Don't they, Pa? If they keep their heads and—" At a loss for further words, Hank reddened and pushed from the table.

"Time for bed, ain't it?" he blurted. Sitting on the floor, he jerked off his boots, threw them in the corner, and got to his feet again. "Tomorrow I'm gettin' enough wood if I have to take the wagon clean back to the Ozarks!"

A pounding at the door brought Hank around on his heels.

"Strange, a body bein' out in this weather," Pa said at the table.

The rest of the Hedins came to their feet, silent and rigid with wondering. Pa cleared his throat and started toward the door. Hank fell in close behind him.

"Who you be?" Pa shouted, his hand hesitating above the latch.

There was a shuffling noise outside; then a man's voice twanged, "Name's Barton. Boney John Barton. Tarnation, mister, open up. We're near froze to death."

Hank edged to one side where, if need be, he could easily reach Pa's squirrel gun cradled on pegs over the door. He gasped as the door came open, and two big, snow-covered figures stumbled inside. Behind them, the snow was still falling. Hank drew back as one of the white figures bolted straight for him. "What—?" he yelled, nearly falling over a chair as he tried to keep away from the hand reaching for him. "What are you tryin' to do?" he gasped.

Then he took notice of the hand and saw that it was almost as familiar as his own. An image of blackness, with the feeling of a warm hand leading him to a bright light, flashed across Hank's mind. His glance darted upward to the face. Pale blue eyes under frosted brows look back at him, twinkling. A big nose poked over a woolen scarf wound around the head—

A strangling sound tore from Hank's throat. *"It's him!* Bigger, Bigger Stokes—it's you—you are back! Where you been—what happened—take your coat off—" Hank reached out to help but Bigger pummeled him affectionately in the ribs and Hank socked him back, laughing until tears burned his eyes.

Panting, they drew apart and looked at one another. "I can't believe it!" Hank said through an aching throat. He helped Bigger take off his coat, then shoved him into a chair. He took the woolen scarf Bigger unwound from his blonde shaggy head. Hank chewed his lip and his Adam's apple worked furiously. At last he could say to his grinning friend, "Bigger Stokes, you fool, 'bout time you showed up."

The next few moments became a happy blur. Only one thought loomed, gigantic, in Hank's mind: BIGGER IS HOME AGAIN.

Mamma was shaking Hank's arm. "Hank. Hank, I'm trying to get Bigger to the table to eat." She laughed. "Move out of the way, Son. Bigger is all right. But our company is hungry. Hank, move!"

"Eat? Oh, all right," Hank stammered. "C'mon, Bigger." He motioned toward Bigger's old place at the table. "Mama," he moaned, "just cornmeal mush? Can't they at least have some mulberry preserves for sweetenin'?"

"'Course. I had that in mind, myself. Get them down for me, Hank."

From a chair, Hank searched the far corner of the cupboard where Mamma stored her precious preserves. One jar. Mamma's last.

"It's all right," she hissed. "Give it to me."

Climbing down, Hank took a good look at Bigger's companion. Boney John Barton was tall, rangy, and so crippled it hurt to watch him move. He scratched his gray head and took a chair at the far end of the table. "This is right kind of you folks," he drawled. "Now that my craw is thawing, I reckon I could eat a bear. You, too?" He grinned at Bigger, who nodded vigorously.

Pa sat down again at the head of the table and Hank hurried to his place next to Bigger. For a few moments they said nothing, although Hank itched with questions, as the newcomers devoured the bowls of mush that Mamma and Johanna kept refilled. About every third mouthful Bigger would turn and grin at Hank and Hank would grin back.

Finally, Boney John drawled, "I reckon you folks would like to know how the boy and me come to be here, an' what we been up to. I'll tell ya—" His voice trailed off as he began to search his pockets.

Hank squirmed impatiently as Boney John pulled out a Bull Durham tobacco sack and papers and proceeded to roll a cigarette. Bigger grasped Hank's arm in a gesture that said as plain as anything for Hank to give the old man time. Hank grinned at Bigger and shrugged.

"I'm a wild horse wrangler," Boney John broke the waiting silence. "Used to be the best, before I got crippled. My territory lies a lot further west of here, most times. But I heard tell of a wild herd or two north of Goodland, an' I come to look things over. I found the boy, here," he jabbed a thumb in Bigger's direction, "tryin' to run them mustangs down on foot."

Horses! Bigger had left—on purpose—to find the herds of wild horses Pa had talked about when they first came—He had gone away to do that without letting him know—Hank's incredulous thoughts were interrupted as Boney John went on.

"The young'un come near to doin' it, too. Him quiet as an Indian, no cussin' or nothing."

At that, Bigger grinned broadly at Hank, and his eyes flashed with an excitement Hank had seldom seen in them. Bigger motioned for Hank to listen to the old wrangler and Hank nodded, glad there was someone to talk for Bigger.

"The boy and me worked together," Boney explained. "I got the know-how when it comes to wild horse catchin', but I'm crippled up 'cause one bad winter I warmed my feet in the ashes of my campfire—" He broke off, and shook his grizzled head. "There was enough life in them coals to burn my boot soles off—my feet froze." He took a long drag on the cigarette and said, "But that ain't what I was fixin' to tell ya."

Hank leaned forward, propping his elbows on the table. Pa, too, looked to be all ears. In the background, Hank could hear the quiet sounds of Mamma and Johanna putting the younger ones to bed. Then Mamma and Johanna came to sit and listen, too.

"There's some mighty fine animals running wild up in the Smoky Hill country," the wrangler told them. "Years ago, immigrants movin' to the Oregon Territory lost a thoroughbred now and then. Those tame horses that got away took up with wild ponies. Plain, ordinary wild horses are just two colors: The leader will be black and his mares almost always red roan. The good horses gone wild might be bay, iron-gray, or white—"

It was obvious to Hank that this was not what Bigger wanted the old man to tell them. He had something else on his mind. Something he wanted Hank to know, now. "What?" Hank asked, in a private whisper to Bigger. "What's the matter? You're twitchin' like a coyote covered with fleas."

Bigger stood up. He turned to the wrangler and motioned toward the door. Then he went to get his coat from behind the stove, and motioned for Hank to get his.

"What's your hurry?" Boney John asked Bigger in exasperation. "It's blizzardin' out there. Awright, if you just can't wait 'nother minute, g'wan, show 'im! I ain't movin' my poor feet from under this table, myself."

As he pulled his boots on and drew on his coat, Hank's pulse raced. If what Bigger was about to show him was what he thought—it was worth going out into the worst storm in history for! But they would need a lantern. Hank's voice shook as he asked for it.

Outside, it had stopped snowing. The air was clear, and the moon showed a bright white world. Hank waited for Bigger to lead the way to the barn, as if he had no idea that was where they were going.

Before the barn door was open, Hank could see that a long, impossible dream was coming true. "You brought them?" he whispered huskily. "You caught them yourself for us, Bigger? All the time I talked horses and cowboyin'—it meant a lot to you, too, didn't it?"

Bigger nodded, pride in every line of his long body as

he went into the barn and stomped the snow from his boots. Hank followed suit, an aching grin plastered on his face. It was slightly warmer inside the barn from the body heat of the animals.

At first, the small barn appeared to be full of horses. But there were only three besides Lucy and Sal. One was black, looked tame, and was probably owned by Boney John, Hank decided.

The other two were shaggy and wild-eyed; their ears twitched nervously at the sight of the boys. They tried to back away as Hank and Bigger advanced, but were hobbled with rawhide thongs and didn't go far.

Bigger pointed to the nearest pony, a red roan, and patted his chest. Hank understood that it was Bigger's own. "She's somethin' to look at, I'll grant you that," Hank said, his voice thick with awe. "Pretty as a rose." His heart pounded as Bigger clutched his shoulder and pushed him gently toward the other filly, a dark bay with a white, fan-shaped mark in the middle of her forehead.

"Mine?" Hank asked, his voice breaking. She shied as he reached a hand toward her. "Fan?" he said softly. "Can I call you Fan?" The little horse tossed her head in a proud way that instantly warmed Hank inside. He had the feeling he could never take his eyes from her finely tapered head, beautiful black mane, her strong body, and trim legs. His!

"Bigger," Hank said, swallowing hard as he faced him, "Bigger, there ain't never been a friend like you. I —" How could he thank him? First, Bigger had saved his life, back when he was lost in the cave. Then he had agreed to come with him on the journey west. Now he was giving him a pony, a beautiful horse all his own. "B-Bigger, don't never go away again without letting me know. I've got to pay you back someday, some way."

The look that Bigger returned was long and serious and slightly tinged with fear. Then he smiled. Chaw Varber, Hank thought wordlessly. Bigger was thinking about Chaw Varber just now. Thinking, maybe, that I helped him get away from Varber. A shiver raced up Hank's spine as it came to him that Bigger did not know Varber was alive and staying nearby.

Hank brushed the back of his hand over his eyes. "We —we better get back to the house," he said unsteadily. He waited as Bigger checked the ponies' hobbles and patted them. As he stared at the back of Bigger's head, Hank's throat tightened. There was still trouble ahead for his friend, plenty of it. And Bigger had no idea that it was so.

Chapter Ten

Hank's shivering, later in bed, was only partially due to the cold. He pulled his quilt tighter about him, but it did no good. All evening, from the moment he remembered that Bigger did not know Chaw Varber was alive and close by, Hank had wondered in a frenzied way what he was going to do.

"Ain't nothin' gonna happen to Bigger 'long as he's with us," Pa had insisted in a whisper when Hank drew him away from Boney John's stove-side yarning. Hank had shaken his head, miserable, unable to understand Pa's lack of worry.

One by one, Hank cautioned the family not to speak of Chaw Varber in Bigger's hearing. Now Hank released the quilt. He listened to the deep breathing of the others in the room; Bigger, Boney John Barton, and the young ones. All asleep. Hank sighed and rolled quietly out of bed. It would be daylight soon. He *owed* Bigger and that was that.

He did not know what he would do when he got to Chaw Varber's shanty. But Hank's blood raced with a satisfying excitement that he was about to do *something*. He dressed and stole from the house.

In the dimness of the barn, he saddled Lucy, and after a longing, sidewise look at his unbroken pony, Fan, he was on his way.

Under the overhang of Jimson Ridge, a few yards from Varber's shack, Hank ground-reined Lucy. When he had left home, he had slipped into his pocket a few pieces of beef jerky that Boney and Bigger had brought. He nibbled a piece nervously, trying to build his courage before facing Chaw Varber.

The dull sky gradually lightened. Hank scooped up a handful of snow to wash down the jerky that stuck in his fear-tightened throat. He wondered, in a moment's panic, whether Varber was even here, then decided the bad weather would no doubt keep him in.

At last, a tiny cloud of smoke lifted from Varber's chimney. Hank waited a while longer. The wet snow squeaked under his boots as he moved toward Chaw Varber's door; the giddy feeling in his stomach bloomed. He knocked.

Chaw Varber was in his underwear. His yellow eyes stared dully at Hank. A thumbless hand went up to push the long black hair away from his face.

"Morn—in'!" Hank's voice cracked. "H-how are you?"

Varber shook his head, his expression bewildered. Like a turtle's, his head suddenly came forward on his shoulders. "What're you doin' here?"

Hank stamped his feet to warm them, searching his mind at the same time. "I—ah—I'm p-payin' a call. Mamma—Mamma's been wonderin' how you're doin'.

Bad weather—you bein' down a while back—" His voice trailed away.

Varber stood there, then finally stepped back. "Aw'right, come in," he said, but his voice was alive with suspicion.

Hank entered, almost choking from the stench of the un-aired cabin and dislike for the owner. He took a chair and stared at the floor while Varber dressed. He was here. *But what now?*

"Whur's the medicine? And food?" Varber broke the silence. "Your Mamma sent some, di'nt she? She's a good neighbor. I been hankering fer bread and soup like she made and left with me, ever since I been at death's door and it brought me back."

"Uh, what?" Hank stalled. "Oh, uh, I'm supposed to bring that—next time." He searched his pocket. "I—I brought you some beef jerky. Yeh, here it is." He held out the dark brown curls of beef.

"That ain't much!" Varber snarled, taking the jerky and tossing it onto the table.

"It's near all we have!" Hank wanted to protest. A vision of his mother, so bone-thin she hardly looked like herself anymore, swam up before him and he half-rose.

"Where'd you git beef jerky, anyways?" Varber questioned. "Don't see it aroun' here fur as I know."

An explosion went off in Hank's mind. Now he had done it! What could he say about the jerky that wouldn't let Varber know Bigger was home? "A—a mustanger brought it," he mumbled, settling back in his chair. In the back of his mind the seed of an idea was starting to grow, but Hank couldn't see yet where it might lead.

"Mustanger!" Chaw Varber exclaimed, his yellow eyes

wide. "In these parts? Ain't no wild horses around here." The Scarecrow slammed a skillet onto the stove and began to carve slices from a chunk of salt pork. He laid out four eggs.

Seeing the food, Hank almost strangled on his anger. He slid to the edge of his chair and sat up stiff and straight, suddenly knowing what he would do and say. But he would have to be careful. He made his voice steady. "The—the wrangler had been in—in Colorado. He was on his way to—to Indian Territory," Hank fabricated, sweating slightly. "Since he was—was goin' through anyway—he brought us a—a message. *From a friend.*" Hank made his last few words almost inaudible.

Varber turned slowly. His eyes glinted like a cat's in the dark.

He smiled. "A message? From that boy? From Bigger Stokes? You finally heard from him!"

"I didn't say that!" Hank protested. The story wasn't going to be hard, after all, and it would be more than worthwhile if it would save Bigger's life. Hank shook his head. "No. Not him," he insisted. "It was somebody else. A—a friend of *Pa's* working—" his fingers dug into his thighs as he tried to think, "as a cook's helper in a—a minin' camp." He held his breath.

"A mining camp," Varber purred. His thumbless hands clawed at the air. "Whereabouts?"

Hank put on an air of disinterest. "Uh, where? Oh, 'round Denver. I disremember exactly where Pa said his friend was." He stood up and moved toward the door. "I reckon I can tell Ma you're not doin' too poorly. She's a real worrier when it comes to the lookout of folks." He lunged through the door.

"Wait!" Varber cried, scrambling after him.

Hank pretended not to hear. "S'long," he yelled, plunging through the snow to where Lucy waited.

Going home, Hank found a small hackberry tree downed by the wind and snow, and he dragged it along. No one questioned where he had been, evidently taking it for granted that a search for wood would be his only reason for being out.

"Hank, t'won't work. Do you think the man's a fool?" Pa hooted when Hank told him privately what he had done. "Falsifyin' ain't gonna cure nothin'."

Hank wondered. Might be Chaw Varber would swallow his bait and believe the story that hinted that Bigger Stokes was in Colorado working in a mining camp. If Chaw Varber didn't take the bait, then he had made no gain at all in protecting Bigger.

HE HAD TO KNOW. TWO DAYS LATER, RABBIT-HUNTING with Bigger, Hank made a wide circle, alone, toward Jimson Ridge and Varber's place.

Wary, his footsteps loud in his ears, Hank found the shack empty. A sigh slipped from him. Chaw Varber was gone. His belongings were gone. Only the filth of the man's quick leave-taking remained. Hank rushed outside and breathed deeply of the sweet, sharp air.

"Yah-hooo!" Hank shouted and tossed his hat at the sun. Still grinning to himself, he retrieved the hat and sloshed through the melting snow toward where Bigger was hunting on the south end of the farm. It would take nigh onto forever, Hank surmised, to search all the mining camps 'round Denver.

~

OFTEN DURING THE COLD WINTER, HANK COULD HAVE sworn that spring would never come to the Kansas prairie, but it did. Days of sunshine followed days of warm rain. Then more sun and more rain. The weather's promise helped when Pa went to the Pillar bank for a loan big enough to get the farm off on the right foot at last.

On Jimson Ridge, above Varber's abandoned, rotting shack, the jimson weed bloomed white once more like bits of the fallen clouds that scudded across the blue sky. The prairie was velvety-green with new grass, but Hank saw that Pa's wheat was even greener.

He said it aloud to Bigger as they jolted homeward one day with a wagonload of sloshing water barrels. "Green. Everythin' is green, ever'where you look." He chuckled the deep man's laugh that had come to him sometime in the months past. "Even our ponies!"

Bigger nodded and grinned.

Hank sobered, anger warming his neck. "If we didn't have to spend all our time ploughin', plantin', and haulin' water, we could ride 'em more and they wouldn't be so spooky." With the scraps of time he and Bigger had been allowed, after Boney John's departure for a friend's in Goodland, they had worked with the ponies. Patting and stroking—getting the animals used to being handled, led, and finally ridden, according to the crippled wrangler's directions.

"We got the job half-done," Hank grumbled on. "They let us ride 'em if the notion suits 'em." Fan shied too easily. More than once a bobbing cottontail or fat bull snake in her path had caused her to send him sailing over her head.

Hank turned to Bigger, beside him on the wagon seat. A trickle of sweat ran down Bigger's face from under the blonde shaggy lock that hung limp against his forehead. "That Smoky Rose of yours is going to take off flying one of these days," Hank complimented his friend. "She's the fastest pony alive, Pa says. An' the way she tries to jump everythin'!"

A broad grin filled Bigger's face.

Hank's deep chuckle grew to a roaring laugh. "How'd it feel," he choked out, "jumpin' Mamma's washtubs in the backyard the other day?" Hank could still see the look on Mamma's face. Mamma had insisted that the little red horse would be clearing her clothesline next.

Hank changed the subject. "Getting hotter, ain't it, and only just into June. Pretty soon it will be hot enough to fry grasshoppers right where they sit."

Bigger nodded and mopped a sleeve across his brow. Watching, Hank saw his arm come down slowly, his pale blue eyes narrowing into a hard stare down the road ahead of them.

Hank looked. It was a man, he decided, after a moment's study of the moving figure etched against the horizon.

Hank's mouth went suddenly drier and he ran his tongue over his lips. It can't be him! he cried inwardly. That ol' Scarecrow is a far piece from here, traipsin' around Colorado. Unconvinced, Hank's heart thundered in his ears. Sweat ran like cold little rivers under his clothes.

It could be Chaw Varber. After the Scarecrow didn't find Bigger in Colorado, and for sure he wouldn't, what would stop him from coming back here? Hank remembered with cold dread that Varber had gone to a lot of trouble to follow them from Missouri.

"He's turnin' in the lane to our place," Hank said in a hollow voice. "There's somethin' queer on his back. A— a chest—big trunk—if the feller is—if it's somebody we know I can't tell."

Bigger's face showed curiosity and nothing more. Hank shuddered. As far as Bigger knew, Chaw Varber had died in that flash-flood last spring.

The team voluntarily picked up speed as they neared home and their feed box. The wagon wheels turned faster; the water barrels rocked and splashed. Hank mopped his brow. He wanted to pull up the reins, turn Lucy and Sal around, head them west, and just keep going. He clutched the reins tighter and craned his neck to see everything he could about the man.

Wasn't he too tall to be Varber? And more solidly built? The stranger's suit was coated with dust. A suit? Varber wouldn't be wearing such a nice-fitting suit. His rags were always loose and flapping around him.

Hank leaned back, a relieved sigh coming up from the very depths of his being. It wasn't Varber. *This time.* He began to laugh, a sound that was weak and weird even to his own ears. Bigger turned to stare at him, his brows rising in question.

"Ain't nothin'," Hank explained, shaking his head. "Ain't nothing 'cept I was just thinkin' that—that body up there is pretty funny-lookin' with a trunk for a head."

Bigger grinned and gave Hank's shoulders a hard shove.

The man heard them and turned around. Hank swallowed the last of his fear and waved. "Mister, want a ride? C'mon, get on the wagon."

The fine-featured face looking up at them was flushed from the heat. The young man smiled. "S-sure enough," he panted. "Like to." He stumbled toward them and both boys came off the halted wagon.

"Stand still," Hank said. "We'll heft your trunk onto the wagon with the water barrels. Bigger, you take that end." The trunk was not as heavy as Hank had thought it might be, but it was heavy enough that the owner had difficulty straightening his shoulders after they had taken it from his back. The trunk thumped loudly as they put it down. Bigger climbed in after it.

In the driver's seat again, Hank eyed the stranger, who rubbed furiously at his shoulders and neck. "You come far?" he asked.

"Far enough that I would like to go no farther," came the weary answer. As they started to move, the young man doffed his gray felt hat, shook the dust from it, and combed his fingers through his curly brown hair.

Watching, Hank thought immediately of Johanna. She would like this good-looking stranger. "How'd you come to be walking, carrying your trunk?" he couldn't resist asking.

"I had a horse and buggy," the stranger said ruefully. "I stopped to rest under a tree. Took my trunk out of the buggy to change my clothes and get a book to read. I fell asleep and my horse ran away, buggy and all. Back to Wisconsin, I suppose, where I got her."

The young man broke into Hank's sympathetic chuckling to further explain that he had been working as a peddler, a horse-and-buggy merchant, through the Midwest. But he didn't like it. He wanted to go back to his former profession of teaching and was looking for a school.

"I got a sister, Elsa, who is downright book-crazy. She'll be glad to see you, especially if you got books in that trunk. Johanna will be glad, too." Hank sneaked a look at Bigger. Bigger's white-lashed eyelid dropped in a broad wink. This feller they were bringing home was just a natural, perfect, stand-up match for Johanna, and Bigger saw it too, Hank thought.

"By the way, my name is Ted Risinger," their rider said.

"My name is Hank Hedin." Hank poked a thumb over his shoulder. "His name is Bigger Stokes. He lives with us, practically my brother, though no real kin."

"You are probably too old for school?" Ted Risinger said, reaching back to shake Bigger's hand.

Turning quickly, Hank saw Bigger point to his mouth and shake his head. "He can't talk," Hank explained quietly. "We don't go to school. I finished eighth grade last year in Missoura. I don't know about Bigger—" Seeing Bigger squirm self-consciously, Hank said abruptly, "Here we are. Whoa, Lucy, Sal." He motioned toward the stone house. "C'mon in, Mr. Risinger, and meet my folks. Bigger, we can unload the water in a bit."

Hank sniffed the air appreciatively. Mamma was baking bread. Good. Mamma's spring fryers darting about the yard weren't quite big enough to eat, but some would land in the skillet anyway, Hank believed, when Mamma and Johanna laid eyes on Ted Risinger.

"How do, Mr. Risinger," Mamma said when Hank introduced them. "This is my daughter Elsa. The twins are Clover and Dixie. In the cradle is baby Lou Ella."

Mamma's eyes shone proudly as she said, "My big girl doin' dishes is Johanna."

Hank watched, trying to control a grin that threatened to stretch his whole face out of shape. Satisfied with the warm look of interest that Johanna exchanged with Ted, he motioned to Bigger. "We better get the water unloaded. Mamma," he said pointedly, "if you want me an' Bigger to catch three or four fryers, we will."

WHEN THE WATER BARRELS WERE IN THEIR PLACE UNDER the overhang of the back porch, the chickens caught, and the horses turned loose in the pasture, Hank and Bigger each took up a hoe and joined Pa cultivating the corn. "We got company, a schoolteacher feller, at the house, Pa," Hank told him. "Ma's fryin' chickens for dinner."

Pa's calloused hands released the cultivator for a minute. He drew his ragged bandanna handkerchief from his pocket and mopped his brow. "Good." He looked over his fields and house and his eyes glowed. Hank remembered the same look on Pa's face the morning he had decided to settle in Kansas.

"Things *are* good, aren't they, Pa?" Hank stopped hoeing to ask. "Mamma's flock of chickens, the new orchard, the garden, the well ready for the windmill, the crops all green and fine."

"Couldn't be better, Son," Pa said, turning his warm smile full on Hank. Then Pa looked at Bigger and shook a fist affectionately at him. "You boys—you boys—" He fell silent as though searching for words to voice something he considered very important. He stroked his red beard.

"You young fellers been a big help; I want you to know that," Pa went on. "I knowed you ain't hankered to be Kansas farmers. An' you don't have to settle for it, if it ain't what you want. You're both gittin' big enough to decide for yourselves. After harvest, if you're still set on headin' on West—"

Pa was telling them they could leave if they wanted! Hank gripped the hoe handle and exchanged a look of surprise and delight with Bigger.

"—One thing," Pa was saying, "before you decide. Look way off yonder." He pointed west. Hank looked at the vast swells of bluestem-covered pastureland rolling on forever beyond their property line. "I'm goin' into cattle-raisin' as soon as I can," Pa said. "Already talked it over with the bank. And Boney John Barton, he is interested in partnerin' with me. We'd need a couple men, cowhands with ponies—"

For a few seconds, Hank wondered what Pa was talking about. Then he knew. "You're sayin'—you're talkin' about Bigger and me, right here?" Hank stammered. He looked at Bigger and saw that he looked eager.

"Think it over for now," Pa urged. "Ain't no hurry."

Hank nodded. "We'll see, Pa. We'll see." Even as he said it, Hank knew inside that their answer would probably be *yes*. Cowboyin'—at home. He was surprised at how good it sounded.

The fruitful, work-loaded but happy days stretched into summer. Ted Risinger helped, and proved with endless mistakes he was not a farmer. In the fall, he would move into Pillar to teach the school there. From all the signs, he would take a bride, Johanna, with him. Watching Ted and Johanna together made Hank think of

Zoe Vonna and his heart would hammer a bit faster. He might call on her, he decided, whenever he was in Pillar visiting his sister and new brother-in-law.

In the meantime, there was the harvesting. One late afternoon, when the hay-cutting was finished, Pa agreed that Hank and Bigger had a pleasure-time coming, and could go swimming before the creek dried up completely.

Leaving Fan and Smoky Rose tied in a thicket of pawpaw, Hank and Bigger examined the creek for a place to swim. In several places, the creek bottom showed, dry and cracked, but at last they found a hole, about four feet deep and twenty feet square.

"Last one in is a yellow-bellied bull snake," Hank crowed, skinning out of his overalls as fast as if they were full of bees. Even so, he saw Bigger belly-land in the muddy green but cooling water the same instant his own body struck it.

"Whew," Hank cried, laughing, settling his body into the mud of the creek bottom. "Feels good, don't it?" With the flat of his palm he sent a spray into Bigger's happy face. "Reminds me of a sayin' Pa knows about the Missoura River: 'Too thick to drink but too thin to plow.' Reckon that makes it just right for swimmin', huh, Bigger?"

Something in what he said caused a strange, pained look to cross Bigger's face, as though he was looking back in time to a memory that hurt. Then the look was gone and Bigger was again smiling.

Hank wanted to ask about it. Maybe it had to do with the Missouri River. There was that fresh-water clam shell that had bothered Bigger a lot—but Bigger would get hot under the collar like he always did when he asked too many questions, Hank decided. It was too good a day to fight. Hank laid his cheek in the water and, with long, clean strokes, swam away from Bigger.

In the west, the sun was starting to set, turning the water and their bodies to pink-gold as they swam. They dressed, finally, and were about to go, when they decided to make a slide on the bank. In the half-dark, they splashed the clay and smoothed it until it was slick as butter. As they romped, their overalls became just as slick.

"Wahoo!" Hank yelled, running up out of the water on a rougher part of the bank. He gave Bigger a shove that sent him spinning, arms and legs floundering, down the bank into the creek. Hank sat at the top of the slide, snickering.

Below him, Bigger wasn't laughing. Hank stared, disbelieving, as Bigger thrashed, went under, came up, went under again. "What—?" Hank started to question, when he heard a sound behind him. His neck prickled as he saw Bigger suddenly start to half-run, half-swim, up the creek. Hank turned.

He felt no surprise, only the sickest kind of fear he had ever known. In the dim light he saw a flapping figure getting off a mule.

Chaw Varber was back.

Chapter Eleven

H ank watched Chaw Varber advance for only a second, and then he was flying down the slippery bank into the creek to follow Bigger.

"Stop! Wait now!" came Varber's vicious order.

Hank considered. Ought he to turn back and face the Scarecrow alone, and stop him if he could? No, Bigger might need him close with him, to get away. Hank gritted his teeth and kept going. His legs fought the shallow water with every ounce of strength they had. There was a soft, frantic splashing ahead of him. Bigger. Behind him he could hear Chaw Varber churning along. The Scarecrow was going to follow them right up the creek!

"Keep going, Bigger," Hank encouraged. "Git to your Smoky pony quick as you can."

The light from the setting sun disappeared as they moved. In the dark behind them Chaw Varber screamed, "Bigger Stokes, stop! You can't git away! I waited long 'nuff. Now I'm—"

Hank's mind automatically closed against Varber's

threat. "We can beat that ol' Scarecrow," he croaked. "Keep going, Bigger."

He could hear Bigger running now on dry creek bed. He reached it himself seconds later and grabbed for Bigger. His friend clutched Hank's arm in a death-tight grip and they raced up the creek bank together.

"Up there, right there," Hank choked out. He snatched both ponies' reins free. "Get on your Smoky pony, quick, Bigger. Here, Fan, steady, girl. Here we go!" He pressed his knees into Fan's warm sides. "Ride for home, Bigger, home."

"Come back here!" Varber shrieked. "You can't git away!"

The beat of Fan's hoofs matched the pounding of Hank's heart. He looked back, but could see nothing. Yet he knew Varber would not be long getting out of the creek.

"Show 'im, Fan," he hissed to the little pony. "Show 'im there ain't a mule alive or anything else that can run as fast as our little mustangs." Hank's heart swelled with exultation as he bent low over Fan's neck. Smoky Rose and Bigger were so far ahead, he could scarcely hear them.

They would make it home, where Pa could help. They had to. Pa was right about the lie. It hadn't done any good. This festerin' sore between Chaw Varber and Bigger ought to have been cleaned out and cleared up a long time ago, Hank told himself. This night, it was going to be!

The way from creek to home had never seemed so long. Hank could hear Varber's mule braying, as if in pain, and knew the animal was probably being beaten.

At the sod barn, Hank threw himself from his horse,

and ran inside after Bigger. One look at the boy's face as he came out of the gloom into the moonlight flooding through the window told Hank that Bigger would not be much help.

"Stay out of sight, Bigger. Stay in here and don't move. I ain't gonna let that Scarecrow get you now." Hank snatched their coiled lariat from the peg by the door and went outside.

He would yell to Pa for help now but that might turn Varber away, putting off what had to be done. Hank took deep steady breaths and waited for the Scarecrow.

Soon, he heard the stealthy plop of the mule's hoofs coming around from the back of the barn. Hank readied the loop of the old rope; his fingertips itched to make the toss. In the pale light, he saw Varber come around the corner of the barn and halt the mule. The click of Varber's tongue was almost imperceptible; then, the mule was moving again in Hank's direction, closer and closer.

Hank made a swift rotation of his wrist. The rope sang around his head, then swished through the air. A Commanche war whoop burst from him as he felt the tug of Varber's unsuspecting body inside his loop. "Pa!" Hank screamed. "Pa, come!" He jerked the rope tight, and ran forward to whip the rope twice more in a circle about Varber, before yanking the Scarecrow off the mule to the ground.

Hank leaped on Varber to hold him down. The Scarecrow lunged under him like a maddened bear. He couldn't hold him long! "Pa," Hank yelled again, "help!"

Varber threw Hank off and came up from the ground screaming. Hank sidestepped his booted foot, gripping the rope. He was aware of the ponies whinnying their terror. The dogs, Ullie and Snoozer, circled him and

Varber snapping, snarling, and barking furiously. Would Pa never come? Was he deaf? Hank worried frantically.

Hank danced, looking for a chance, then jumped on Chaw Varber from behind. It was like jumping into the middle of a tornado. He couldn't handle Varber alone. "Help!" he yelled. In that instant he saw a large, over-alled boy-figure dive from the dark doorway of the barn to help drag Varber to the ground. *Bigger*.

"Pa," a voice yelled. "Pa."

Hank froze; his heart almost stopped. That soft, twangy voice wasn't his!

"H-Hank?" the voice said uncertainly.

He'd never heard it before—a stranger's voice saying his name? Calling for Pa?

No, not a stranger. *Bigger,* yelling! Real words, out loud!

A never-before feeling enveloped Hank. His hands went weak and he could no longer hold Varber at all. "Thunderin' toads, Bigger, you're talkin'. You're talkin'—!"

He watched Bigger get to his feet. He loomed there, hands outstretched. "Hank?" he repeated. "Hank. Hank!"

The Scarecrow took that moment to renew his enraged battle against the ropes that held him. Hank saw it in the eerie wash of silver moonlight, but, still dazed, he couldn't move. Suddenly, Chaw Varber's hands and arms came free. Hank knew, in the back of his mind, that the old hide rope had broken, but still he could do nothing.

Chaw Varber lunged at Bigger. The dark, grotesque hands reached for the boy's throat. The Scarecrow screamed, "You took it that night. You got it! Where is it?"

"No! Leave him alone!" Hank shouted, suddenly himself again. He went for the back of Varber's legs, desperation giving his body sledge-hammer force as he hit. Varber grunted sharply and landed on the ground with a loud thud. This time he didn't get up.

"What's goin' on out here? Can't a body git any sleep? Hank, Bigger, I figgered you boys got in a long time ago and went to bed. Who's that on the ground?"

"Pa," Hank cried, "Bigger can talk."

"What!"

Bigger dropped to the ground, as though his legs would no longer hold him. He covered his face with his arm, but his muffled voice, faltering, came through. "He —killed—them. He—killed—Ma—and-Pa."

"C'mon, Bigger," Hank said huskily. "C'mon in the house. Pa can take care of that mean ol' Scarecrow now. You don't have to run from him no more."

"He killed—my Ma and—Pa," the soft voice kept saying.

It was the next forenoon, after a bruised and squawling Chaw Varber, tightly bound in strips of canvas wagon cover, was handed over to the sheriff in Pillar, before Bigger could say anything more.

In the Mayfields' cool front room, across the street from the jail, Hank, Bigger, Pa, Mr. Mayfield, and Zoe Vonna sat drinking lemonade. "Can you tell us now, Bigger?" Hank encouraged.

Bigger nodded, but said nothing for several seconds. He fidgeted on the sofa, then began, "We was clammers. Ma. Pa. Me. We lived in a houseboat. Missoura River. Ioway. Our—our work was rakin' up fresh-water clams. We sold the clam shells to a company that made 'em into pearl buttons. One day, my—my Pa—" Bigger hesitated, then went on, "he found a big *pearl* in a clam. Though to find a good pearl of any size is rare."

Bigger looked in the direction of the jail and stammered, "He—he—"

"Chaw Varber?" Hank quietly helped.

Bigger's pale blue eyes thanked Hank. "V-Varber was a clammer, too. He wanted—pearl—tried to take it from Pa. Pa give me the pearl." Bigger's voice sank to a bare whisper. "Pa told me—to swim—other side of the river, and not—not let Varber have it."

For several minutes, Bigger was silent. Then, he whispered in a choked voice, "From the other side of the river I saw—saw the fire, the houseboat burning. He—he did it. Ma and Pa inside. I couldn't help—so far away. Pa and Ma, trapped—I kept screaming and screaming. Leastways, I think I did. But when I stopped, I couldn't say nothin', no more, after the fire."

As he listened, Hank's breath came in jerks. Across the room, he saw the glistening wetness on Bigger's cheeks, just before his own sight clouded over. "When —?" he tried to ask, but his voice failed him.

Bigger looked at him. "About—about two years ago, I think."

"Oh, no!" Zoe Vonna cried out.

"You been runnin' and hidin' from him all this time!" Pa exclaimed. "All the way from Ioway!"

Hank looked at the wall, fighting the fierce ache in his throat. No wonder Bigger couldn't talk. No wonder he always looked to be scared of his own shadow. Chaw Varber probably knew Bigger saw him do away with his folks and was after him for that too, besides the pearl.

Mr. Mayfield cleared his throat. "Chaw Varber will

be sent to Iowa to stand trial for the murder of your folks. You won't ever have to worry about him again."

"Let's git that pearl to the bank now, for safekeeping," Pa sighed, getting to his feet.

Bigger drew a fist-sized pouch from inside his shirt, the same pouch Hank had noticed at the cave when Bigger had agreed to go West. Hank drew in his breath as Bigger shook two objects out into his palm. One was the shell Hank had found for Clover; the other was a large, white pearl.

"You know you're practically a rich man, don't you, Bigger?" Pa asked as everyone drew close for a look at the gleaming pearl.

Bigger grinned and shrugged. His voice, still not steady, but pleasant, explained. "I—never once thought— about it that way. The pearl was—just something I had to keep running with, like my Pa—told me to do. He said— not to let Chaw Varber get—it— and that's the only thought—I've had about it."

Hank shook his head. Bigger hadn't been running and hiding for two years just because he was scared. More than that, he was doing his dead Pa's bidding. "I'm glad it's all over," Hank said, heaving a sigh, "Glad I found you in the cave, or rather that you found me."

Pa moved toward the door, and the boys followed.

"Next time you're in town, bring the whole family over for supper," Mr. Mayfield invited.

"We will," Hank answered, his eyes meeting Zoe Vonna's.

Before leaving town, Bigger insisted on a stop at McCracken's store to buy presents for Mamma and the girls. Then they were on their way, Pa driving the wagon in which he had hauled the bound Scarecrow to town, Hank and Bigger mounted on Fan and Smoky Rose.

"I s'pose now that you're a rich man, Bigger," Hank said after a while, "you'll be wantin' to live in Kansas City, or someplace. Or maybe go back to Ioway. You got other people there?"

Bigger shook his head.

"Well, then, how about it?" Hank asked. "Whether we stay home or go on further West, do you still want to cowboy with me?"

Bigger nodded.

Hank turned hot when he realized that Bigger was teasing him by not talking. Then Hank had a flash of an idea. He could get Bigger to speak! "Do you think that ol' pink horse of yours can beat mine in a race to home?" he asked.

Hank almost fell off Fan, laughing, when Bigger answered:

"THUNDERIN' TOADS, YES!"

A look at: Willow Whip

From award-winning author Irene Bennett Brown comes a heartwarming story of a young girl determined to make it possible for her constantly moving farmer family to buy a farm that she has come to love and wants to live on permanently.

Could the Faber family really afford a farm of their own? Could they stop moving from place to place? Her father has almost given up hope, but for Willow Faber, the only dream worth having is a farm of their own.

The Fabers are tenant farmers. They move almost every year trying to find a better place. But no farm will ever compare to the one Willow calls "The Ranch." Once a Pony Express stop, it is old, but solid and pleasant, and Willow is willing to do everything she can to make it theirs.

For a long year Willow does little but plan and work and save, pushing herself—and her family—to the brink, earning herself the nickname "Willow The Whip." She sacrifices everything, including all of the things she had hoped to gain by staying in one place. Only near disaster helps her understand what she has lost and all that she still has to gain.

Follow this young heroine in a wild and wooly adventure that is a testament to the triumph of the human spirit and strong will.

AVAILABLE JANUARY 2024

About the Author

Irene Bennett Brown is an award-winning author who enjoys using Kansas—where she was born—as background for her historical novels. Previous to her ten novels for adults, Brown authored nine young adult novels. *Before the Lark* won a Western Writers of America Spur Award, was nominated for the Mark Twain Award, and received other honors. Her other YA novels include *To Rainbow Valley, Run from a Scarecrow, Skitterbrain, Willow Whip, Morning Glory Afternoon, Answer Me Answer Me, I Loved You Logan McGee,* and *Just Another Gorgeous Guy.*

Her most recent Nickel Hill series include *Miss Royal's Mules, Tangled Times, Somebody's Business* and *One True Deed.* All are adult sequels to *Before the Lark.*

She lives with her husband, Bob—a retired research chemist—on two fruitful acres along the Santiam River in Oregon.